Payback

Also by Solomon Jones

Payback

Solomon Jones

The Return of C.R.E.A.M.

MINOTAUR BOOKS
NEW YORK

Published in the United States by Minotaur Books, an imprint of St. Martin's Publishing Group

PAYBACK. Copyright © 2009 by Sola Productions, Inc. All rights reserved. Printed in the United States of America. For information, address St. Martin's Publishing Group, 120 Broadway, New York, NY 10271.

www.minotaurbooks.com

The Library of Congress has cataloged the hardcover edition as follows:

Jones, Solomon, 1967–
    Payback : the return of C.R.E.A.M. / Solomon Jones.—1st ed.
      p. cm.
    ISBN-13: 978-0-312-34838-0
    ISBN-10: 0-312-34838-X
  1. Women ex-convicts—Fiction.   2. African American women—Fiction.
3. African Americans—Pennsylvania—Philadelphia—Fiction.   4. Philadelphia
(Pa.)—Fiction.   5. Mothers—Death—Fiction.   I. Title.
    PS3560.O5386P39 2009
    813'.54—dc22

                                                                        2008034171

ISBN 978-1-250-83472-0 (trade paperback)
ISBN 978-1-4299-9485-9 (ebook)

Our books may be purchased in bulk for promotional, educational, or business use. Please contact your local bookseller or the Macmillan Corporate and Premium Sales Department at 1-800-221-7945, extension 5442, or by email at MacmillanSpecialMarkets@macmillan.com.

First Minotaur Books Trade Paperback Edition: 2022

10 9 8 7 6 5 4 3 2 1

To Philadelphia,
the city that inspires my stories

ACKNOWLEDGMENTS

First, as always, I thank God for granting me the talent and the determination to write. I am awed when I see where He has brought me and humbled when I envision the path He has in store for me. I am grateful to those who continue to believe in me, including my best friend, my wife, LaVeta. To my children, Eve, Adrianne, and Solomon, I am proud to be your father. To my parents, Carolyn and Solomon, thank you for shaping me, loving me, encouraging me, and placing in me the very best of yourselves. To my aunt Juanita and my grandmother, Lula, thank you for always being there with prayers, belief, and support. To my friends Harold, Susan, and Ben Jacobs, thanks for always providing wise counsel. To Congressman Chaka Fattah, thank you for being a great teacher and friend. To my agent, Manie Barron, thanks for believing. To my buddy Dana, thanks for being there. To my friends at the *Philadelphia Daily News* and Philadelphia Media Holdings, thank you for sharing my vision. And to you, my readers, thank you for your undying support. You are the reason that I write.

Payback

1.

Fluorescent lights shone against Karima Thomas's face as spectators in the crowded courtroom craned their necks to get a glimpse of her.

She was accustomed to such stares. Her cocoa-colored skin, absent of makeup except for a simple lip gloss, was flawless. Her nails were painted with a pearl-colored polish that matched her Bottega Veneta clutch. The white linen suit she wore hung perfectly from her shoulders. Her silky brown hair was pulled back in a braided French twist.

It wasn't her beauty that caused people to watch her so closely. It was her fame. In the two months since Mayor Jeffrey Tatum's murder, she'd become a household name, and everyone knew her story.

It had begun on the first of May—two weeks before Philadelphia's primary elections—when the mayor was gunned down and Karima was blamed.

The police had searched desperately for Karima while she and her boyfriend, Duane Faison, crisscrossed Philadelphia in pursuit of the mayor's real killer. When they finally found the shooter, he tried to escape, and Duane was shot in the confusion.

Karima was arrested in connection with that shooting and the murders of two politically connected drug dealers. Duane's deathbed confession in two of the three shootings—and the fact that Duane had been shot with more than one gun—convinced a judge to free Karima on $10,000 bail with the stipulation that she submit to electronic monitoring.

When Karima and her lawyer emerged from the courtroom following that decision, the media was waiting.

"Did you kill Duane?" a reporter shouted as she and her lawyer walked through the parking lot.

"Are you guilty?" yelled another reporter while cameramen jockeyed for position.

Karima stopped suddenly and turned to face them, her emotions still raw from Duane's death two days before.

"We've all done things we're not proud of, but I'm not a monster, and I won't let you turn me into one," she said, holding back tears as the cameras rolled. "I loved Duane. He knew it, I knew it, and that's all that matters."

Through the rest of May and most of June, prosecutors sifted through evidence. The media told stories about the beautiful suspect and the drug dealer who'd died defending her. Karima focused her attention on her mother, Sharon Thomas, the recluse who'd come out of hiding to defend her daughter. The two of them took walks along the tree-lined streets of Sharon's affluent neighborhood, watching spring give way to summer as paparazzi photographed their every move. They laughed at silly jokes. They cried for Karima's loss. They loved each other.

Along the way, Sharon resolved to make up for the time they'd lost to her years of seclusion. "I promise I'll be there for you, no matter what happens in the case," she told her daughter more than once.

Now it was July, and today, Sharon and the rest of the world would learn Karima's fate. The preliminary hearing had begun at eight o'clock in the morning, and its outcome would determine whether the case would go to trial.

The wooden benches in the pine-and-marble courtroom were filled to capacity. There were cameras from truTV. There were reporters from every news outlet. There were people from both sides of the law.

Karima's Aunt Marilyn, the disgraced City Council president who'd been implicated in the City Hall corruption probe, was in attendance. Councilman Richard Ayala was there, though he'd refused to press charges against Karima and Duane for attacking him during their quest to solve Tatum's murder. The families of the two drug dealers who'd been killed were in the back, exchanging hostile stares with the police and federal agents who were scattered among the sheriff's deputies who normally worked in the courts.

All of them had one thing in common: Karima. As the room's recirculated air grew thick with the smell of stale sweat baked beneath television lights, the spectators hung on every word, waiting to see what would become of the woman who'd changed Philadelphia forever.

They listened as witnesses testified about the mayor's extra-marital affairs with both Karima's Aunt Marilyn and her mother, Sharon Thomas. They listened as others implied that Karima was just another in a long line of women in her family who would stop at nothing to get what they wanted.

Karima listened, too. She heard people she hardly knew describe her as a whore. She heard others label her a lifelong criminal. She heard gasps when political insiders gave twisted accounts of her relationship with the mayor. With each lie, Karima's anger grew stronger. She managed to hold her feelings in check—feelings that had been threatening to boil over since Duane's death two months before.

The feelings ran from anger to grief and back again. In between there was the emptiness she'd always held inside. When Duane was alive, she had told herself that he had filled her void. Now that he was gone, she knew that she'd never felt truly complete. If she couldn't find her missing part now, she never would. That was why she needed to go free. When the judge went to her chambers to consider the testimony, Karima considered her future.

She'd already been cleared in the mayor's murder because of the ironclad case against the mayor's chief of staff, who'd been implicated by his co-conspirator, Karima's father, Bill Johnson. Prosecutors had also decided to drop the murder charges in the drug dealers' deaths due to Duane's deathbed confession.

Now she had only to beat the weapons and aggravated assault charges connected to her violent hunt for the mayor's real killer, and the murder and attempted murder charges that had been filed against her in connection with Duane's death. If she did, the story that had been framed by the press as the Romeo-and-Juliet saga of a beautiful good girl and a rugged bad boy would finally end. Things had rarely been that simple for her, nor would they be that simple now.

"Karima," her lawyer said, tapping her lightly on the shoulder. "Get ready. The judge is about to come in."

She looked at him with the hardness that had lingered in her eyes since Duane's death.

"Okay," she said, taking a deep breath before turning around to look for her mother, Sharon Thomas, who'd kept her promise and been there through every day of Karima's ordeal.

When Karima didn't see her, she panicked. "Where's my—"

"She's in the hallway talking to the young man she was sitting with," her lawyer said, patting her arm to calm her. "She'll be right back. Don't worry."

Karima had seen the two of them sitting next to each other earlier. The man looked familiar—hauntingly so.

However, the man wasn't important to Karima. Her mother was. Over the past two months, Karima had watched Sharon's transformation from a recluse to a woman who'd decided to live again, a woman who'd put her own fears aside to help prove her daughter's innocence. In spite of everything that had happened in the past, and no matter what happened today, Karima would always love Sharon for changing. More importantly, she knew that her mother would always love her, too.

"All rise!" said the bailiff, stirring Karima from her thoughts. "The Municipal Court of Philadelphia is now in session, the Honorable Myra Weaks presiding."

Karima stood up. The judge, a stern woman with cowrie shells in her salt-and-pepper dreadlocks, sat down.

After telling the spectators to be seated, the judge glanced at Karima with a look that appeared to carry the promise of swift punishment.

"Will the defendant please rise?" she said in a strong, clear voice.

Karima and her lawyer stood.

"After carefully considering the testimony that was offered here today," the judge said before pausing to look over the top of her glasses at Karima, "this court finds it unfortunate that there's nothing in the criminal code to cover stupidity. If there were, I'd lock you up for going to jail for a drug dealer, going back to him when you were released, and putting your life on the line for him when he clearly didn't have your best interests at heart."

"You don't know anything about him," Karima murmured before her lawyer or anyone else could stop her.

The judge angrily snatched off her glasses. "What did you say?"

The gallery erupted in loud gasps. Karima's lawyer squeezed her hand and gave her a look that begged her to be quiet. But there were now two angry black women in the room. Neither was about to remain silent.

"I said you don't know anything—"

"Please forgive my client, Your Honor," her lawyer said, cutting her off.

"I don't need forgiveness," Karima said, her voice rising slightly. "I need her to know this isn't about Duane. It's not about posturing for these cameras. It's not about putting our relationship on trial. As far as I'm concerned, the only fact that's come out of this is that Duane Faison loved me better than any man ever could. He loved me so much that he took a bullet for me."

"No, he took a bullet *from* you, Ms. Thomas," the judge snapped.

"That was an accident," Karima retorted.

"None of us knows that for sure," the judge said. "And while this court would love to consider your version of the facts, the truth of the matter is that the evidence presented here today is enough to hold you over for trial on the charges of aggravated assault, illegal possession of a firearm, and attempted murder. The evidence doesn't support the murder charge . . . yet."

The spectators' voices rose to a loud hum and the judge banged her gavel. "I will have order in this court or I will clear everyone out of here including these cameras!"

The noise in the courtroom subsided and the judge leaned forward in her chair. "Karima Thomas, it is the decision of this court that there is sufficient evidence to take this case to trial. You will be processed at the Philadelphia Industrial Correctional Center. Because this court considers you a flight risk, bail is set at one million—"

A loud scream ripped through the air. It sounded as if it had come from the hallway.

Sheriff's deputies rushed out the door as chaos erupted. A few seconds later, Karima's worst fears were realized.

"Someone call an ambulance!" one of the deputies yelled. "Hurry!"

The judge banged her gavel as people began to run toward the confusion. The cameraman from truTV tried his best to make his way into the crowd.

Karima turned around and saw what was happening. Then she jumped the railing and began pushing her way through.

"Ms. Thomas, stop right there!" the judge shouted.

That was when everything seemed to slow down for Karima.

She looked to her right and saw reporters squeezing out the door. To her left, she saw a sheriff's deputy darting toward her. Federal agents and police detectives were spilling into the hallway in an attempt to restore order. Karima would not be stopped.

She tossed people aside with a strength that belied her size as she scrambled across the room. She pushed past the sheriff's deputy who dared to stand in her way. When she reached the hallway and knelt down, her heart stopped at the sight of Sharon Thomas lying motionless on the floor.

Sheriff's deputies surrounded Karima, but refused to intervene when they saw her kneel at her mother's side.

"Get up, Mom," Karima said, feeling like a helpless little girl. "Please get up."

Sharon didn't move. Karima's eyes darted back and forth. Her breath came in great heaving gasps.

"Mom?" she said, shaking her mother's shoulders. "Mom!" she screamed as grief washed over her. Karima felt like she was the victim, but that feeling made her want to fight all the more.

Blinking back tears, Karima stroked her mother's hair. "I love you," she said with a furrowed brow and quivering lips. "I'll find whoever did this to you."

Sharon looked up at her daughter with eyes that told her not to seek revenge. Karima saw what her mother was trying to say, and answered her mother's unspoken plea.

"You know I've always done what I had to, Mom. That's why I'll find whoever hurt you."

A look of grim determination swept over Karima's face as she stroked her mother's hair. "Seeing you grow these last two months has been . . ." Her voice broke, and she paused to gather herself, because Karima refused to cry. "Remember your promise, Mom. You said you would be there for me no matter what happened."

Sharon looked up at her daughter and tried to smile. She couldn't, though. She was too weak.

Karima reached down and cradled her mother's head in her lap. As Sharon closed her eyes and lapsed into unconsciousness, Karima's white linen suit grew red with the blood that leaked from the small wound at the base of her mother's neck.

Karima's self-control gave way to rage.

"Mom!" she screamed. "Mom!"

The sheriff's deputies moved in. One of them slapped a handcuff on her left wrist. Karima began to scratch and claw at them with her free hand. As the deputies grew in number, Karima's aggression became more pronounced.

"Mom!" she screamed as she kicked a male deputy in the groin. "That's my mother!" she shouted before snatching at a female deputy's hair.

Finally they put a knee in her back and forced her down until her screams were muffled by the floor. As she continued to struggle beneath the force of six people, they cuffed her other wrist and dragged her to her feet. That was when the paramedics arrived.

Karima grew eerily calm as she watched the rescue workers administer CPR to her mother.

"We'll get the bail!" her lawyer shouted as the sheriff's deputies pulled her back into the courtroom. "You'll be out by tonight!"

Karima ignored him. As they took her to the corridor that led to a waiting prison van, she scanned the courtroom for the man who had sat next to her mother.

He was gone. Sharon might be, too. As Karima thought of her

mother's life slipping away, she felt something sticky running down her wrists. Things were just as they'd been on the day Duane had died. There was blood on Karima's hands again.

"Why do you keep doing shit like this?" Jocelyn Lynch yelled as she wagged her finger in her husband's face, hoping that the pain in her voice could make him care again.

Kevin Lynch wouldn't respond. He couldn't anymore. His refusal to take his daughter to a freshman orientation at the University of Pennsylvania was just the latest chapter in an argument that had raged throughout their marriage. His job as a Homicide captain was his identity. That left little room for anything else—including his wife of seventeen years and the daughter who'd grown up virtually without him.

"Are you listening to me, Kevin?" she said with a hand on her hip and attitude in her voice. "Our daughter needs you, and you're telling me that just this one time out of a hundred and fifty, you can't let someone else handle it?"

"The Tatum murder is my case, Jocelyn," he mumbled as he tied his tie and picked his gun up off the bedroom dresser. "I need to be there."

"Your *case*?" she asked with a mix of sarcasm and disgust. Then she closed her eyes, took a deep breath, exhaled slowly, and spoke in a softer tone. "You don't get it, do you?"

Kevin took note of the calm that had replaced Jocelyn's rage. When she was calm, as she'd been when they'd met at the University of Pennsylvania nearly twenty years before, she was at her best.

He still remembered the resolve she'd shown when they were

both at Penn and his grandmother died. She'd calmly told him how blessed he was to be alive. Then she pushed him to look at his own past and let it go. He remembered the way she'd helped him to shake off the ill effects of being raised in the rough-and-tumble world of the East Bridge projects. He remembered that woman and wondered where she'd gone, and as he thought of the way he'd treated her over the years, he wondered where he'd gone as well.

"Do you remember the miscarriage?" she said, breaking into his thoughts.

He felt a pang of guilt as he recalled the child they'd lost, and all he wanted to do was escape.

"I can't talk about this now," he said as he tried to leave the room.

She blocked his path and forced him to look her in the eye. "We both cried when we lost that child, Kevin. We cried because we loved each other. We cried because something that we made together died that day. Do you remember that?"

He wanted to answer, but couldn't. Her chestnut-brown eyes were filled with too many accusations. The strength in her voice was too challenging. Yes, he remembered, though he didn't want to.

"After that happened, we promised each other that we would give Chantal all the love that other child would've gotten. We said we'd put our family first."

"You think I'm not doing that?" he said angrily. "I've spent the last seventeen years fighting to get rank in the department so we could have a better life. I've managed to do it, too, even with the racism and the cronyism and the politics and all the other bullshit. But it's never good enough, is it? Even with everything I'm dealing with on the job, I still have to come home and deal with you."

"No, Kevin," she said, smiling as if she felt sorry for him. "You don't have to deal with me. You don't even talk to me. You just come home with the weight of the world on your shoulders and expect me to open my legs and make it go away."

"That's not true," he said, sounding exasperated.

"It *is* true!" she said sharply. "There was a time when you wanted more than that, and I was happy to give it to you. If that's all you want now, that's okay. The minute you lowered your expectations, I lowered mine, too. That's why I don't wait around for anything from you, Kevin. Not affection, not emotion, not anything."

"Then why do you keep doing this?" he blurted out in frustration.

"Because I want you to love our daughter as much as she loves you!" she said as tears welled up in her eyes.

"I do!"

"You can't!" she yelled as a single tear rolled down her cheek. "If you did you would know that everything she does is for you. She didn't graduate from Central High with a 4.0 to impress her friends. She didn't choose Penn over Princeton because I went there. She did it because *you* went there. She wants you to approve of her, Kevin."

"I do!"

"Then prove it! Notice her. Love her. Tell her she's worth more to you than some silly-ass job!"

Lynch stood there with his mouth agape, asking himself how

it had come to this. In truth, he knew the answer. His work required him to be a hero rather than a man. It was exciting. It was sexy. It was dangerous. Home was something else altogether. It was a place where he was married to a woman who'd come to despise him, and that was the very last place he wanted to be.

He reached up and rubbed his temples between his thumb and forefinger, closed his eyes, and told her what she wanted to hear. "I'll take her down to Penn's campus today," he said as his Black-Berry began to ring.

She looked at the phone with disgust. "Sure you will," she said sarcastically.

He connected the call and listened as the voice on the other end explained what had happened at the courthouse. Seconds later he grabbed his badge from the dresser.

"I gotta go," he said, pushing past her and walking toward the bedroom door. "We can talk about this later."

"There might not be a later, Kevin," she said as he opened the door and saw his daughter standing there.

He stopped in his tracks as he looked into eyes as beautiful as Jocelyn's, and a face etched with the same pain. He immediately knew that his daughter had heard the argument. He could tell by the way she looked at him, as if she were waiting for him to utter the words that would make everything all right.

Lynch had no such words. He reached down, took his daughter's face between his hands, and kissed her gently on the forehead.

"I love you, Chantal," he said without waiting for a response.

As he ran down the stairs and out the door, he called the lieutenant on the scene to get further details, then jumped in his car and peeled out. As he did so, he thought of Jocelyn. Perhaps she was right.

Maybe later would never come.

The sound of sirens filled the air as every available unit was called to the Criminal Justice Center. Foot patrol officers ran the block from City Hall to 13th Street, while bicycle officers pedaled feverishly toward the scene from all points in Center City.

When the arriving cops waded into the crowd of officers, witnesses, lawyers, and defendants who were gathered outside the building, the result was instant chaos. Defendants came face-to-face with their accusers. Cops on their way to testify in other cases were called on to maintain order, and as cameramen transmitted live shots of the action, a woman shouted four words that made everyone hit the ground: "He's got a gun!"

A group of officers charged from every direction, and the thirty-something black man she'd pointed out was swiftly and brutally subdued while cameras recorded every blow.

A woman who was with him screamed for them to stop. A child nearby cried out for her mother. The blows rained down until the man was still. As he was handcuffed and snatched up from the concrete, an officer wearing rubber gloves reached into his pockets.

He removed a Trio, and then a wallet. He thumbed through it and found a faculty identification card from nearby Community College of Philadelphia.

The man was a college professor. There was no gun.

When the crowd saw the bloodied man and the officer holding nothing more than a wallet, the mood turned even uglier. The officers began to push the cameramen away. The people—screaming about racism and brutality—began to close in on the police. Meanwhile, Lynch screeched to a halt, jumped out of the car, and immediately forgot all about home. This was his element, and in it, he was all that he wanted to be.

His brown bald head glistened with sweat. He was tall and walked with a confidence that eluded him at home. Here, he was a man of importance rather than a failure.

People stood aside as he calmly walked through the crowd, past the cameramen, and up to the officers involved. "Who's in charge here?"

A sergeant stepped away from the others. "I am, sir," he said, moving close to whisper in Lynch's ear. "We thought he had a gun."

"Let him go," Lynch said as the other officers looked on.

"But, Captain, we—"

"I said let him go. Get his name and address and tell him where he can file a complaint. I need you and your officers to get control of this crowd and secure the front of this building."

The sergeant nodded toward one of the officers, who removed the man's handcuffs as the other officers began to move the crowd back.

"Any word on what's going on up there?" the sergeant said, looking toward the top of the Criminal Justice Center.

Lynch followed the sergeant's gaze. "Karima Thomas's mother was stabbed outside the courtroom. They don't know if she's gonna make it."

"Any suspects?"

"Apparently there was a guy who was sitting beside her right before the two of them went out to the hallway. He disappeared in the confusion. The building's on lockdown until we can get out a description and interview witnesses."

The sergeant nodded toward a prisoner transport van parked on the corner of 13th Street. "They just brought down Karima Thomas. The van's getting ready to—"

"Thanks," Lynch said, cutting him off as he started toward the van.

He hadn't seen Karima since taking the gun from her after Duane was shot in the Crystal Tea Room two months before. In a way that made him feel uncomfortable and wrong, he was looking forward to seeing her again.

Perhaps she could make him forget the trouble at home. At least, that was what he hoped as he moved toward the van. That was only part of it, though. In truth, Lynch wanted some insight into Karima Thomas. He wanted something that would confirm what he'd always believed—that Karima would never do any real time. Her face was too beautiful, her story too perfect, her presence too powerful. Of course, with the case now going to trial, it was entirely possible that he was wrong.

Lynch flashed his badge at the deputy in the front seat. The deputy rolled down his window and Lynch nervously twisted his wedding ring as he stuck his head in and saw her for the first time in two months.

"Karima," he said, his tone sympathetic. "I need to talk to you."

She folded her shackled hands against her bloodstained pants and looked at him, her eyes red with rage. "There's nothing to talk about," she said. "You arrested me. I'm here. What more do you want?"

"I want the truth," Lynch said, staring at her in spite of himself.

Karima smiled bitterly. "Somebody stabbed my mother today," she said in measured tones. "I don't know who and I don't know why. I'll find out, though, because I want the truth a whole lot more than you do. If you know anything at all about me, you know I won't stop until I find it."

"Who do you think would want your mother dead, Karima?" Lynch asked.

She stared out the van's front window. "You're the Homicide captain. Isn't it your job to find that out?"

"Do you know anything about the man who was sitting beside her up there?"

"I've never seen him before," Karima said, in a tone both angry and controlled.

Before Lynch could press her further, three cameramen spotted the van. In seconds they surrounded it and the questions began to fly.

"Karima, how will you cope with your mother being attacked in the courtroom?" asked a rotund reporter from Channel 6.

"What will you do now that the case has been held over for trial?" added a fresh-faced woman from Channel 10.

"Have you gotten over the death of Duane Faison?" added a reporter from the *Inquirer*.

The cameras were all around the van, preventing it from moving. Karima's face was almost completely obscured by the van's gated windows. That didn't stop them from trying to get to her.

"Karima!" a photographer said, pushing through the crowd and snapping a picture of her.

He was about to take another shot when Lynch rushed up to him and knocked the camera from his hand.

As the man bent to pick up his camera, Lynch whispered into his handheld radio and a cadre of cops appeared. They quickly moved the reporters out of the way.

"Get her out of here," Lynch said to the deputy who was driving.

As the van pulled off in a hail of flashbulbs, Karima looked out the window at Lynch—the man who'd knelt beside her when Duane's life streamed out in a flow of blood.

He'd treated her tenderly even then. From the way he had looked at her, it seemed that he wanted to do far more than that now.

2.

The curtains moved as a morning breeze and the echo of a faraway gunshot blew in through the open window of the North Philly rooming house.

Clad in a sweat-soaked wifebeater and oversized basketball shorts, Chuck lay against his twin-sized bed and watched the curtains move. The breeze was enough to maintain his interest. The gunshot wasn't. He'd seen and done enough with guns to last him a lifetime. Not even the nine-millimeter beneath his mattress was of interest now.

It wasn't that Chuck had abandoned the game. He couldn't afford to. For the past month and a half, he'd eked out a living as a low-level dealer on the corner of Stillman and Jefferson. His boss was a man known as Heads, a former pro football prospect from a Division II black college whose career was short-circuited by injury. Heads was imposing at six-five and 290 pounds. But he was too flashy too often, and his ruthlessness had earned him far too many enemies. Though Heads had filled the void Duane had left and wanted desperately to be like Duane had been, he hadn't learned to be low-key, like Duane. Chuck knew that it would only be a matter of time before Heads was cut down.

As Chuck sat on the bed, fingering his nine-millimeter and eyeing the $5,000 package of crack he was supposed to put on the streets in an hour, he knew that he had no intention of dealing for Heads that day. In fact, he had no intention of ever dealing again. His bag was already packed, and after the meeting that would take place in a few minutes, he planned to be gone. It hadn't always been that way for Chuck.

Just two months before, while working for Duane and his brother Ben Faison, Chuck was earning a thousand dollars a day slinging crack while occasionally doubling as Duane's driver.

He'd taken Duane to cigar bars and high-end restaurants on Philadelphia's Walnut Street. He'd taken him to the Ritz-Carlton and the Four Seasons. He'd taken him to the Union League—the conservative men's club that until recently had been exclusively white.

The trips were always the same. Chuck would pick Duane up in a nondescript car, and the two would ride in silence. When they reached their destination, Duane would get out and slip a sports jacket over a white collared shirt, his tall frame, chocolate skin, and cornrowed hair easily distinguishing him from the rich white men all around him. Ninety minutes later, Chuck would return and take Duane back to North Philly.

Chuck never knew why Duane frequented those places, and he didn't ask. In fact, he never asked questions about anything, and he never let ambition get the best of him.

He had survived three years in Duane's operation by obeying those simple self-imposed rules. Things changed for Chuck when he watched Duane and Ben torture another low-level dealer named T-Bone who'd stolen crack from them.

The memory of the brutal attack haunted Chuck in his waking hours, and frightened him in his sleep. Even now, there were nights when Chuck wakened in a cold sweat at the sound of T-Bone screaming in his dreams.

He still remembered sitting in the abandoned house, watching them beat T-Bone to the edge of unconsciousness. He still remembered the way they'd carried him from the house, naked and covered in his own blood. He remembered the hush that fell upon the corner as they loaded him into the trunk of an old car. More than anything, he remembered Duane lifting a box high into the air and emptying dozens of writhing snakes into the trunk while T-Bone sobbed in horror.

"Don't ever try to take mine from me!" Duane had said as the others looked on, terrified. "'Cause I don't let go that easy!"

T-Bone disappeared, and Chuck knew that it could have easily been him. Shortly after that, Chuck began trying to figure a way out of the game.

With little education, no family other than his abusive foster parents, and no guile to think of a way out, Chuck believed that he was stuck there. Things changed when a man he'd known as a child tracked him down.

It happened on the same day that Duane, Ben, and their street manager, Rob, wiped out rival drug dealer Glock, and the rest of the 29th Street crew, ending the war between the two corners before it could begin. Mayor Tatum had shown up at the crime scene, forcing a rare raid by police who would otherwise have done nothing.

With Duane and his lieutenants long gone, Chuck and ten other dealers from 25th Street were rounded up and questioned at police headquarters. No one could offer much more than what the police already knew—that Duane ran the corner along with his hotheaded younger brother, Ben, and his longtime confidant, Rob. Chuck wasn't compelled to tell them anything more, either. The next day, when the mayor was killed, the priorities changed. They let Chuck go.

As he was leaving police headquarters—tired and unsure of what to do next—a brown-skinned, almost pretty man in a pin-striped gray suit sidled up to him and called him by name.

Chuck looked confused as he stared at the man. Then recognition swept across his face. "Troy?" he said after seeing shades of the boy who'd spent two years with the same foster family as Chuck. "Where you come from?"

"I just got back into town," Troy said in a high-pitched voice as he smiled almost seductively. "I heard about what happened and I thought I might be able to help you." He paused and spoke in a conspiratorial whisper. "Actually, I thought we might be able to help each other."

"Don't nobody just pop up talkin' 'bout they wanna help you 'less they want somethin'," Chuck said, eyeing him suspiciously. "So why don't you just tell me what you want?"

Troy reached into his pocket, peeled off five hundred-dollar bills, and held them out toward Chuck. "I want some information, that's all."

Chuck looked at the money, and his mind went back to their

childhood. He saw a much younger Troy with money in his hands, and remembered joining with the other boys in the neighborhood to take it from him. Though they'd lived in the same foster home, the two of them had never cared for each other like brothers. When Mr. and Mrs. Williams beat Chuck for his thug-like manner or beat Troy for his effeminate ways, neither of them ever stood up for the other. Chuck knew that Troy wasn't out to help him—not after they'd been enemies as kids.

Chuck cocked his head to the side. "What, you a cop now?" he asked curiously.

Troy laughed. "No. I'm just trying to catch up on some things. I knew you needed the money and I thought you might be able to help me. You know, as a favor."

It was Chuck's turn to laugh. "I can't do you no favors, man," he said as he pushed past Troy. "But I need you to do me one. Get the hell away from me."

Troy went away. Duane's drug operation crumbled, and Chuck went to work for Heads, the first dealer to step into the void that was left by Duane's fall.

Heads liked that Chuck had kept quiet about Duane's operation when under pressure by police. He also liked that Chuck had experience on a major corner. Most of all, he liked that Chuck had no other choice.

Heads gave Chuck a package, a nine-millimeter, and the day shift. He paid him half of what he was making with Duane. With nowhere else to go and nothing else to do, Chuck was forced to take what he could get, but he was looking for a better deal. So when Troy came back two weeks later with an offer to pay Chuck in exchange for information, Chuck listened.

Troy wanted to know about every place Chuck had ever taken Duane. He wanted to know dates and times. He wanted to know names and descriptions. If Chuck provided the information, Troy told him, he would make sure that Chuck was taken care of. So far, after their first few meetings, Troy had been true to his word. He'd paid Chuck enough to allow him to build up a nice little nest egg. Today would be their final meeting, and when it was over, Chuck planned to take the money and leave North Philly for good.

A knock at the door stirred Chuck from his thoughts. Quickly, he got up from the bed and placed his gun and the package beneath the mattress.

He looked out the improvised peephole he'd drilled in the door and saw Troy. "I thought you said eight-thirty," an irritated Chuck said while stepping aside to let him in. "You late."

Troy walked in smiling, his red, bow-shaped lips dominating his light brown, hairless face.

"I almost didn't make it at all," Troy said, his voice a bit too high for a man of his size.

"Why?" Chuck asked as he and Troy sat down in rickety chairs on either side of a rusty card table.

"I went to Karima's hearing this morning. There was some trouble and they weren't letting people out."

Chuck nodded as he thought about Karima—the woman he'd known only as Cream. Duane had given up nearly everything for her. In the end, it had cost him his life.

"What you go to the hearin' for?" Chuck asked.

"Let's just say I was curious," Troy said, shifting in his seat and crossing his legs. "But we aren't here to talk about that, are we? We're here to talk about that last piece of information you were going to give me."

"We can talk after you gimme the money," Chuck said.

With a tight smile, Troy reached into the breast pocket of his black suit, took out ten one-hundred dollar bills, and placed them on the table. "Now, I need to know the last place you took Duane before he died."

"I took him across the bridge to Jersey," Chuck said, looking down at the money as he counted and recounted it. "Place called Washington Commons, or somethin' like that."

"When?"

"Probably 'round seven o'clock the day before Cream came home from jail."

"Any idea who he went there to see?"

"Seem like it was this old broad named Regina. I think he met her in City Hall before, too."

"Do you know what they might've talked about?"

"Money, man. All that shit was 'bout money," Chuck said, checking his watch and glancing at his packed bag in the corner of the room. "Anything else? I'm 'bout to bounce."

"No, I think that's it."

"Yeah, I guess it is," Chuck said as he looked at his room for the last time.

Troy stood and extended his hand. "Take care."

"You, too," Chuck said, standing up and shaking hands with Troy, who towered over him. Chuck quickly pulled his hand away when he felt something sticky.

"You bleedin'," he said, looking down at the blood on his hand.

"That's not my blood," Troy said, the bass suddenly evident in his voice. He looked at Chuck and his smile disappeared as his face clouded over with simmering rage.

That look held the anger he'd harbored since the day he'd met Chuck as a child. The rage from the time Chuck had punched him in his nose was there, along with the hurt he'd felt when Chuck had refused to help when Troy was bullied. The look held the betrayal from the time Chuck had joined with two other boys to rob him of his pay from his very first summer job.

The rage in Troy's eyes had been brewing for more than a decade. Chuck saw it and knew someone was about to die in that room. Chuck didn't want it to be him.

Diving toward the bed, Chuck snatched his gun from beneath the mattress, dragging out the package in the process. Troy moved just as quickly, grabbing Chuck from behind. Chuck tried to turn the gun on Troy, but the bigger man wrapped his forearm around Chuck's neck, choking him. Chuck managed to get off two shots as the breath was squeezed from his body. The slugs hit the wall as Chuck continued to struggle. Troy grabbed Chuck's wrist with one powerful hand and squeezed until Chuck dropped the gun on the floor.

"I hate you," Troy whispered as Chuck struggled to break free. "You were the only one who could've helped me when we were growing up, but you helped them to hurt me instead. You watched when Mr. Williams beat me. You laughed when the other kids punched me. You helped them take what was mine."

Chuck's strength waned as he tried to break free from Troy's freakishly strong grip.

"Are you still laughing, Chuck?" Troy asked as Chuck's eyes grew wide with terror. "Is it funny now?"

Troy loosened his grip ever so slightly, and Chuck made a last attempt to break free. As he did, Troy plunged his ice pick into the back of Chuck's neck, gripped his forehead with his palm, and pushed the ice pick slowly into the base of Chuck's brain.

Chuck slumped to the floor as Troy stood over him. He stared down at Chuck's body and savored the moment. Then he wiped the blood from the ice pick and pulled a list of seven names from his pocket. He crossed off Chuck before reaching down and taking the $1,000 he'd just given to him. He ran over to the bag in the corner and rifled through it, looking for the other four thousand dollars he'd already paid Chuck. It wasn't there, so he took the drugs that had fallen on the floor instead.

Quickly, he moved to the room's open window and lifted it as high as it could go. He climbed out and hung by his fingertips, dropping down from the second floor and into a pile of trash in the alley below.

He dusted himself off as he jogged through the alley and emerged on Cecil B. Moore Avenue. He looked behind him and saw neighbors beginning to gather outside the rooming house. Sirens blared in the distance as Troy walked calmly toward the gray Taurus he'd parked just half a block away.

As he got in and drove toward Fairmount Park, Troy felt nothing in the space where guilt should have been. Chuck would have eventually figured out that Troy had stabbed Sharon, and since Chuck was one of the only people who knew Troy well, he couldn't be allowed to live.

Not that it mattered. Troy now had the information he needed to finance and execute the plan he'd put in place more than a year before. All the research, all the planning, all the details would come together now. Troy would finally have the thing he wanted most: payback.

The police arrived almost instantly, as if they knew that this was no ordinary drug-related murder. They were met by a crowd of senior citizens, children, and jobless men who had gathered outside the rooming house where Chuck's lifeless body lay on the floor.

Within minutes, they began to play out the ritual that was repeated far too often in North Philly. Police officers placed crime scene tape in front of the building. Children watched intently as they learned the first of many lessons from the streets. As the crowd milled about, waiting anxiously for the body bag's slow trek down the stairs, police waded in, asking the questions that most had the good sense not to answer.

In this place, where generations of people lived under the twin weights of poverty and one another, there was very little that the neighbors didn't know. The same system of law enforcement that begged their cooperation provided no protection for witnesses. Those who agreed to testify often found themselves on the receiving end of a bullet. While the media cried for people in beleaguered areas to stand up to the criminals, the media didn't have to live next door to killers who had a 50 percent chance of getting away with murder.

Here, in a place where it was nearly impossible to get the

overworked and underpaid police to do so much as issue a parking ticket, there weren't many people who were willing to risk their lives to say what they'd seen. A few blocks away, where dilapidated houses and poor brown faces had been replaced by deeper pockets and lighter skin, things were different. Police enforced every one of the city's codes. Protection was provided with a smile. The new North Philadelphians wouldn't stand for anything less, because if Philadelphia was going to convince more urban pioneers to move to the edge of the 'hood, the criminals would have to learn to respect the dividing line.

The man in the black Mercedes knew that. He sat in his car, which was parked a block away from the rooming house where Chuck had been slain, watching the crowd carefully to see who was talking to the police. After all, this was *his* domain. Police and neighbors alike would have to respect that, or there would be hell to pay.

Heads wasn't a man who would tolerate anything less than total submission. The last time he'd allowed anything remotely resembling disrespect was as a child, when his large skull had earned him the name Heads. Over the years, the man born Anthony Porter had made even his derogatory nickname into something to be feared.

By the time he was sixteen, his body had caught up with his head, he was nearly three hundred pounds of muscle, and he was revered as a star offensive lineman at Ben Franklin High School. After making the All-City Team, he attended Delaware State University on a scholarship and played three years of flawless football.

In his senior year, the aunt who had raised him died of cancer. A serious knee injury scared away the NFL teams that had considered drafting him in the first round, and though he was subsequently invited to several training camps as an undrafted free agent and could have taken that path to the top, Heads had never been treated as less than a star, and he wasn't about to accept anyone's crumbs.

Heads came home to North Philly with grief in his heart and a chip on his shoulder, and he set about making his millions in the streets instead of on the field.

He spent months watching Duane Faison and wishing he could have everything Duane did, including the woman they'd all come to know as Cream. On more than one occasion, he'd considered killing Duane and taking it all. Once, he'd even hired someone to do it. When the shooter missed and was found dead of a gunshot wound the next day, Heads distanced himself from the whole sordid affair.

Duane died before Heads could make another move, so he did the only thing he knew how to do. He bullied his way onto the scene.

Using the same tools he had used as an offensive tackle, he beat his opponents by going lower, moving faster, and establishing leverage any way he could. Once he was able to push them backward, he wouldn't stop until they were flat on the ground. When he was finished, he made sure they weren't able to get up.

That's what he planned to do now.

Reaching into the pocket of his baggy basketball shorts, Heads fished out his phone and dialed the number to the disposable cell phone he'd given to the youngest employee on his payroll.

"What's good, Skeet?" he said to the thirteen-year-old boy who answered on the first ring.

"Hold on a second," said the lanky boy as he tugged at his low-slung shorts and craned his neck to see over the crowd.

With narrowed eyes, Skeet examined the crime scene like he'd seen it all before. Having grown up with dozens of old heads who fed their various vices at his aunt's speakeasy, Skeet had seen more in his thirteen years than most people see in a lifetime. He knew a setup when he saw one. He knew game when people ran it, and thanks to Mr. Vic—the old man who'd spent years as his aunt's on-again-off-again boyfriend—he knew people.

Heads had known from the very first time he'd seen the boy cheat seasoned poker players by dealing from the bottom of the deck during a high-stakes game in the speakeasy that Skeet was a hustler at heart. He'd offered him a job on the spot. He told the boy then, like he told all his workers, that he would die if he ever tried to cross him.

Thus far, the investment he'd made in the boy had paid off in spades. Skeet knew North Philly like the back of his hand, and knowing the neighborhood was what allowed him to give Heads the first real information about the crime.

"The dude that killed Chuck wasn't from 'round here," Skeet whispered into the phone after surveying the crowd. "He had came to see Chuck like two or three times before. Somebody said he looked like some kinda cop, 'cause he was wearin' a suit and drivin' a Taurus."

"Yeah, but where my shit at?" Heads asked in a tone that made it clear where his concerns lay.

The boy looked toward the house and spotted the patrolman

who'd been on Heads's payroll for almost a year. He'd arrived on the scene first, and he'd searched unsuccessfully for the drugs that were supposed to be in Chuck's room.

"It wasn't there," the boy said quietly.

"Fuck you mean it wasn't there?" Heads yelled before taking a breath to calm himself.

The boy didn't respond. There was no need to, since he didn't have an answer.

"Look," Heads said while rubbing his temples. "Far as I'm concerned, whoever killed Chuck took my shit. Put out word that I got ten grand for anybody that find him and bring him to me."

"All right, Heads," the boy said, already trying to figure out a way to claim the reward for himself.

As Skeet melted into the crowd to begin an investigation of his own, the police continued to shuttle in and out of the building where Chuck's body lay.

Heads watched them for a moment before opening the sunglasses holder over his car's rearview mirror. He slowly placed his thousand-dollar sunglasses over his eyes, reached down to turn on a Lil Wayne CD, and made a wide U-turn on Cecil B. Moore Avenue.

His Mercedes cruised down the avenue, with the sound of the bass-heavy Crunk filling the morning air with words that echoed Heads's every intention. As he bobbed to the sound of the profane celebration of drug dealing and murder, Heads leaned back in his seat and relished the opportunity he'd just been given.

Someone had killed one of his dealers and stolen a package of crack. In an ideal world, Heads would've found the killer himself. Now he could let the world know that he was seeking retribution.

When he found the offender and punished him, Heads would finally gain the type of status that Duane Faison had acquired before his death, and no one would dare to challenge him again.

An hour had passed since the courtroom stabbing, and everyone had been ordered back into the courtroom as homicide detectives conducted on-the-spot interviews on Captain Lynch's orders. Blood still stained the hallway. Shock still filled the air. As the detectives questioned and photographed one potential witness after another, one thing became abundantly clear. Almost no one had gotten a clear look at the man who'd been sitting next to Sharon Thomas before she was stabbed in the hallway.

Marilyn Johnson was among those who couldn't describe him. She'd barely looked at her sister during the hearing because she hated being in the same room with her. That was why she'd sat on the other side of the courtroom, with her attention focused elsewhere when the mayhem erupted in the hall.

Kevin Lynch wasn't about to let Marilyn use that as an excuse. After speaking with Karima, he made it his business to come up to the courtroom and personally question the woman most likely to know why Sharon had been attacked.

"How are you?" he asked, sitting down next to Marilyn, who looked ten years younger than her forty-five years, wearing a low-cut blouse and short skirt that showed the assets no one could take away.

"I've been better," she said, her tone dry as she pouted at the blond FBI agent who sat close to her and watched her every move.

"I'm sure you have," Lynch said.

He'd watched her fall hard after her role as a cooperating witness in the federal probe of City Hall was revealed. Lynch knew, however, that Marilyn was still powerful. She had extensive knowledge of City Hall corruption, having served as council president, then as Mayor Tatum's replacement before being forced out because of her involvement in the federal investigation. She was the only member of the politically connected Thomas family who knew the depths of the family's secrets.

For those reasons, she was as valuable to Lynch as she was to Special Agent Dan Jansen. The mature femininity that nearly burst out of her clothes was alluring as well—and it seemed to have a disarming effect on Jansen.

"I hope you don't mind me sitting in on this interview," the FBI agent said to Lynch with a mischievous smile. "I mean, you might be able to get something out of her that I can't."

Lynch made a point of allowing his eyes to linger on Jansen's close proximity to Marilyn. The two looked a little too comfortable together. "Oh, I doubt very seriously that I could get more out of Mrs. Johnson than you."

Jansen's face flushed. Before he could respond, Lynch turned his attention to Marilyn.

"When was the last time you spoke with your sister before today?"

"I haven't spoken to her since she slept with my husband and gave birth to Karima," Marilyn said, sounding annoyed. "What's that—twenty-three years?"

"Have you spoken to any relatives who may have had contact with her in recent months? Anyone who might have any ideas about who she'd been in contact with?"

"There aren't many relatives left, Captain. Other than myself and Sharon there's an uncle in Maryland, my aunt and her husband in Harrisburg, and their son who goes to school in Atlanta." She paused. "My family doesn't talk much."

Lynch jotted down notes as she spoke. "I'll get contact information for those relatives from you a little later," Lynch said. "Right now, I need to know something else. Something that's been bothering me since the mayor was killed."

"What's that?" Marilyn asked.

"Sharon was a recluse before Karima was implicated in Tatum's murder. Everyone I talked to said it was because of what she'd been through in politics; that too many powerful men had taken advantage of her, and when she finally met the man she loved, he turned out to be your husband. She never got over the fact that he chose you over her."

"I guess that's true," Marilyn said, waiting for the other half of the question.

"As bad as that sounds, it just doesn't seem like enough to make someone give up on life," Lynch said, his tone perplexed. "I've always thought there must be something more." He looked at her with an accusation in his eyes. "Is there?"

"How could I possibly know what was going on in my sister's head to make her lock herself away like that, Captain?"

"I would think that if anyone would know, it would be you. Especially since the two of you were so close growing up."

"Well, I *don't* know," Marilyn said, speaking through clenched teeth. "And whatever it was, it hasn't been an issue for the last two months, because she's been out and about living a normal life, from what I understand."

"Did that normal life include a boyfriend?"

"I don't know."

"Did it include any men at all?"

"I don't know."

"Did it include anyone who'd want to harm her?"

Marilyn huffed in exasperation. "I told you that I haven't spoken to my sister in over twenty years. I mean, the woman had a child by my *husband*, for God's sake. I don't know her friends. I don't know her enemies. And I certainly don't know of anyone who would have wanted to harm her."

"So when you say, 'I don't know of anyone,' are you including yourself?" Lynch asked coldly.

"Yes, I am including myself," she said as her eyes bored holes into him. There was a moment of uncomfortable silence as the two stared each other down.

"Look," Marilyn said, breaking the silence. "You know I didn't have anything to do with what happened here today. A roomful of people saw me sitting clear across the room from my sister, and I never went out into the hallway. How could I have stabbed her?"

"You couldn't have," Lynch said. "But who's to say you didn't have it done?"

"That's ridiculous," Marilyn said. She looked at Jansen. Her eyes were asking for his help, and because he was more focused on what was below her eyes than what was in them, he was more than willing to give it.

"I think Mrs. Johnson is done here, Captain," Jansen said, standing up and helping Marilyn to her feet.

Payback

"She might be done for now, but I'm sure we'll be chatting again soon," Lynch said, standing up with them. "That federal immunity she has in the City Hall probe doesn't apply here."

Jansen smiled tightly. "Good luck on your investigation," he said. "Please let us know if there's anything we can do to help."

"Well, there is one thing," Lynch said, glancing at Marilyn before looking Jansen in the eye.

"What is it?"

"I need to talk to Bill Johnson."

"That shouldn't be a prob—"

"Today," Lynch said pointedly. "*With* Karima."

Jansen looked from Marilyn to Lynch, wearing an expression that said it was impossible. They all knew that Johnson was in federal custody while Karima was being transported to county prison. Bringing the two together would take days under normal circumstances, but these circumstances were far from normal.

"We'll see what we can do," Jansen said, then placed his hand gingerly against Marilyn's hip and guided her away.

Lynch watched the way Jansen hovered over Marilyn as he walked her out the door. It looked almost like Marilyn was in charge.

"Detective," Lynch said, calling out to one of his men.

A smallish, brown-haired man with bright gray eyes walked over to him. "Yes, Captain."

"Make sure we know where Marilyn is at all times," he said, looking at his watch. "I think she knows a lot more than she's letting on."

"Yes, sir," the detective said.

The captain's BlackBerry rang as the detective scurried away to carry out his order. "Lynch here," he said.

A voice on the other end said that there had been another ice-pick stabbing at a rooming house at 25th and Cecil B. Moore Avenue. Someone fitting the description of Sharon's alleged attacker had been seen getting out of a gray Taurus with a partial tag of GVU. Dispatchers were about to put out a general radio message with his description and the car's last known direction— west toward Fairmount Park from 25th Street.

"Get every available car out to the park," Lynch said as he ran out the courtroom door. "I'm on my way."

3.

Troy's powerful hands gripped the steering wheel tightly as he drove toward the park and tried to avoid slipping into the past.

He glanced at his hands as he drove, and as he often did, he remembered the terror that such hands had once inflicted upon him.

As Troy's face crumpled with a mix of anger and fear, a voice screamed in his head, "Come here, boy!"

It was the voice of his foster father, calling him to the basement as a child.

"Stop talking to me," Troy said aloud as he stared at the road and imagined the damp chill of the basement.

"Gimme your hands!" the voice said, and Troy felt a pain in his left wrist as he remembered the unrelenting steel of the handcuffs his foster father had used.

"Lemme go!" Troy pleaded in the voice of a little boy. "Please, Mr. Williams. I won't do it anymore!"

"Shut up, faggot!" the man snapped. "You said that shit the last time!"

The sound of clanking chains filled Troy's head as he guided the car toward the park while steering his mind through the memories.

He shivered as he recalled being stripped naked and standing on the cold concrete of the basement floor. He felt a pain near his right hand as he remembered being handcuffed to a water pipe and hung by his wrists. His body jerked as he felt the pain of the thick leather strap against his legs and back.

"What did I do?" Troy whispered as the tears streamed down his face. "What did I do?" he asked again in a louder voice. "What did I do?"

"You lived, faggot!" the man's voice shouted as the thick belt smacked against the little boy's back.

Troy's body jerked once more, and the pain of his past snatched him back to the present.

He sneered as he drove toward his destination, knowing that he was prepared to face those who'd abused him so mercilessly: the foster parents who had beaten him; the father he'd never known; the family that had abandoned him to the social services system.

It was in that system that Troy had endured the terror of the basement, and transformed himself from the timid boy who still lived somewhere in his head. In spite of that system, his brilliant yet troubled mind had carried him to boarding school and through Virginia Tech on full academic scholarships.

Now twenty-three, his body was sculpted muscle, honed to perfection by years in the gym. His face, with its soft skin stretched out over chiseled bones, was plain at first glance, but was beautiful when studied closely. He'd learned to ignore the lustful stares he routinely received from both men and women because it wasn't sex that interested him.

His thoughts, as they had been since he was a child, were focused on vengeance. Everything he did—his job, his education, his life—had been centered on it.

Today he would have the revenge he'd always dreamed about, and he would finally be released from his inner torment. At least, that's what he hoped.

As he guided the gray Ford Taurus through tree-lined Fairmount Park, he reached down and turned up the car's police radio. He smiled as he heard the alert tone that preceded the description.

"Wanted for two stabbings in the last hour," the dispatcher read in a monotone. "Black male, light complexion, six foot three, two hundred twenty pounds. He was last seen driving a white or gray Ford Taurus west on Cecil B. Moore Avenue. The male should be considered—"

Troy turned off the radio and headed toward a road that ran parallel to one of the park's main baseball fields. At this time of morning, the old man would be here. He always was. That was why Troy wasn't surprised when he saw the burgundy van parked beneath a tree along the side of the road.

Pulling up behind it, he saw a man leaning back against the headrest. He couldn't see the passenger, but he knew that one was there, because the man's head moved slowly from side to side, almost in unison with the van's slight rocking motion.

Troy got out of his car with the money and crack he'd gotten from Chuck and walked to the passenger side of the van. When he reached the window, Troy stood there for a moment, looking at the old man's tightly shut eyes and wide-open trousers. The man's lips were parted slightly and he moaned every few seconds, his hips writhing as the scantily clad crack prostitute in the passenger seat sucked him greedily. His hand was wrapped around the woman's matted weave, pushing her head up and down as he moved toward a climax he would never reach.

Troy snatched open the passenger-side door. The woman jumped up, surprised. The man's eyes snapped open. Troy pulled the woman out of the passenger seat and pressed $100 and his car keys into her hands.

"Take that car and get out of here," he said, nodding toward the Taurus.

She hesitated and Troy reached into his pocket and threw her the tightly packed, $5,000 package of crack he'd taken from Chuck. She caught it and her eyes lit up. For a moment, she was frozen with delight.

"Now!" he shouted, and she ran to the car, looking back as the old man tried to drive off.

Troy jumped into the van as it was rolling forward, then reached over and threw it into Park. The prostitute screamed past in the Taurus, skidding wildly around the curving road. As the woman disappeared into the distance, the old man turned slowly toward Troy and his ice pick.

Troy looked at him with disgust. His pants were halfway down his thighs and his penis was semi-erect. His eyes were wet with tears and his lips were dry and white. The only thing worse than the stench the woman had left behind was the sickening smell of the old man's fear. Troy hated him for being afraid. It reminded him of the frightened little boy he'd been. But he hated him even more for preying on the weak. It reminded Troy of the way he'd been preyed upon when he was small.

"Don't hurt me," the old man begged, trembling as he looked from Troy's eyes to the ice pick.

"I won't if you do as I say," Troy said, slouching down in the seat.

The old man nodded.

"Pull up your pants, put the van in gear, and drive through the park—slowly."

The driver did as he was told. They moved through the shaded blacktop beneath the trees. Every few seconds, the sound of humming engines and the pulse of flashing lights overtook them as police cars flew past, no doubt looking for Troy.

"Turn here," Troy said, guiding him through the park toward Kelly Drive, a road that ran parallel to the river.

The old man worked up the courage to say something. "Look, why don't you just take the van and let me out?"

Troy smiled. Then he giggled. Then he laughed uproariously. "You don't even know who I am, do you?" he asked when he was calm enough to speak.

"Should I?"

Troy smiled again. "Pull over here."

The driver complied, pulling into a space on the right side of the road.

"It's been interesting watching you these last few weeks," Troy said wistfully. "Always in the same spot, always the same time of day. Always sitting there with your head back, loving every minute of your little five-dollar blow jobs. I'm surprised your wife lets you out."

"What do you know about my wife?" the old man asked, truly confused.

"You mean you don't know, Mr. Williams?" Troy asked, his smile disappearing.

"How do you know my name?"

"How could I not? You and your wife abused me for two years. Remember? I was too little, too weak, and too scared to fight you then."

The old man stared at Troy's face and the memories came flooding back. He looked afraid.

"I've still got the scars from all those times you handcuffed me and hung me from the water pipe," Troy said as he pushed up his sleeve to show a long black mark winding around his wrist.

"I—I was trying to help you," the old man said, his voice quivering. "I didn't want you to turn out—"

"Shut up!" Troy said, grabbing him by his hair and pushing the back of his head down against the seat.

The old man looked up into Troy's eyes and saw the little boy he had so mercilessly abused. He saw the hurt and the anger. He saw the emotional scars. He saw the madness.

Mr. Williams opened his mouth and tried to scream. Troy's face twisted into a maniacal grin as he raised the ice pick high and plunged it into the old man's Adam's apple. Blood squirted across the van's crushed velour seats as he looked at his victim's twitching hands. He remembered how those hands had tortured him, and as tears welled up in Troy's eyes, he stabbed the old man's hands dozens of times before finally plunging the ice pick into his victim's right temple.

His chest heaving, Troy took off his jacket and calmly wiped the blood from his hands.

After throwing the old man into the back of the van, Troy moved over into the driver's seat and pulled his list of names from his bloodstained jacket. He crossed off the third of the seven names before stuffing the list into his pants pocket. Then he drove north on Kelly Drive while chaos erupted around him.

As soon as she'd rounded the curve and pulled out of sight of the van, the woman driving the Taurus pulled over and loaded her makeshift metal crack pipe with three of the nickel bags from the package Troy had given her. With shaking hands, she reached into her purse and extracted a lighter. Then she held it to the end of the pipe and pulled the smoke deep into her lungs.

Her mouth began to water and her heartbeat quickened. The sound of imaginary whispers filled the car's empty space. A pleasure she hadn't known since her first hit of crack caused her legs to shiver with excitement. As her insides grew wet with the pleasure that came from the smoke, the sound of a police siren caused her to look up.

At first she thought the police car that had pulled up behind her was a figment of her imagination. When the officer jumped out with his gun drawn, she knew that it was all too real.

"Get out of the car!" he yelled.

The woman had no intention of doing so. Without a backward glance, she dropped the hot pipe, scalding her legs, and stomped on the gas as the crack pipe rolled onto the floor.

The cop fired his weapon, shattering the Taurus's back window before getting back into his car to give chase.

The Taurus screamed around the gray tarmac that ran along the perimeter of one of the park's many baseball fields, then skidded left, and flew down a winding two-way road called Reservoir Drive. By then, two more police cars had joined the chase, and all four vehicles were traveling at nearly one hundred miles per hour.

The woman looked nervously in the rearview mirror as the police cars closed in on her. Then she glanced at the drugs on the seat. She knew she had to have one more hit like the last one, and she knew she was willing to die to have it, so she pressed the accelerator to the floor, pushing the gray Taurus around yet another curve and skidding on the blacktop as the sound of wailing sirens filled the air.

She made a sudden right and hit the long block of Diamond Street that served as one of the park's exits, barely missing a little girl and her grandparents as they walked along the edge of the grass.

As she approached the edge of the park on 33rd Street, a police car came from the right and screeched to a halt, blocking the Taurus's path. She skidded and swerved left, clipping the front of the police car before heading north on 33rd.

Police radios blared as commanders tried to give orders to break off the pursuit. The calls for assistance drowned out the orders and the police cars moved even faster.

The Taurus couldn't outrun them, but it matched their speed, its engine humming as the car reached 120 miles per hour. As it sped north, a police car traveling south crossed over and blocked its path, forcing the driver to go west on Dauphin Street, alongside a public bus depot.

A Route 39 bus was just leaving when the Taurus turned the corner. The woman let go of the steering wheel and shielded her eyes as the car plunged into the side of the bus. Within seconds, both vehicles burst into flames.

As fire department sirens wailed in the distance, SEPTA supervisors and police officers ran to the bus, prying open the doors so the passengers could escape. Kevin Lynch pulled up and jumped out of his Mercury Marquis as the last of the passengers ran from the wreckage.

He immediately ran toward the car, but an explosion stopped him in his tracks.

"Get back!" he yelled to the officers who were about to move in to try to pull the driver from the vehicle.

The heat from the gasoline-fueled fire became unbearable. Lynch looked at the car's license plate and saw the charred GVU lettering that had been given in the description. He knew that they'd chased the right car.

When the fire department arrived, extinguished the flames, and pulled the dead driver from the vehicle, it was clear that the chase wasn't over.

Lynch looked into the burned face of the victim and saw that it was a woman. And when a grief-filled scream ripped through the air behind him, he knew that a family member was nearby.

As a Fire/Rescue worker placed a sheet over the body, Lynch turned around and saw a gray-haired woman leaning against a young boy. He walked slowly over to the two of them. "Do you know that woman?" he asked.

The old woman was grieved beyond speech, so she nodded through tears as the young man stared angrily at the sheet covering the charred body.

"That's my mom," he said, his ten-year-old face looking far too young for his age-old eyes. "At least, she used to be my mom before she started fuckin' with that crack."

A single tear rolled down his cheek. "I guess we ain't gotta worry 'bout her trickin' in the park no more."

Lynch bent down to talk to the boy. "Do you know why she would've run from the police the way she did?"

The boy hesitated for a moment before deciding that he had nothing to lose. "My dad used to beat her," he said without a hint of emotion. "One day she shot him and they gave her five years in prison and fifteen years' probation. She was walkin' off twelve more years."

He regarded Lynch with a look that was far too knowing. "Maybe she thought she was goin' to jail," he said flatly. "Maybe she ain't wanna go out like that."

The boy looked at his grandmother, who was still in no condition to speak. Then he took a final look at the sheet covering his mother's charred body.

"We live over there," he said to Lynch, pointing to a well-kept two-story house on a nearby tiny street. "Y'all can send somebody over if you need to talk to us. I gotta get my grandmom outta here."

Unsure of what to say, Lynch simply nodded. Then he watched the boy and his grandmother as they walked back to the house, remembering what it had been like to be raised by his grandmother in the projects. She had always been the one protecting him. He couldn't imagine what it must be like for kids who played the opposite role.

"Captain Lynch!" said a Homicide lieutenant who ran up to him excitedly. "We ran the plates on the car and they came back stolen, but we think the car might be a law enforcement vehicle."

"Philadelphia police?"

"No. FBI."

"Where the hell would he get an FBI vehicle?" Lynch wondered aloud.

"Don't know," the lieutenant said. "We're double-checking the vehicle identification number. We should know in a little bit."

"Keep me posted on that," Lynch said, glancing at the car's dead driver. "And let me know as soon as we get IDs on this body and the one on Twenty-fifth Street. Hopefully there's some connection that'll help us catch this guy before he kills again."

The lieutenant nodded as Lynch took one more look at the body. Just as he was about to turn away, something in the wreckage caught his eye. At first, it appeared to be an automotive part— a fluid container, perhaps—that had melted into a large wad of burned plastic. When Lynch looked again, he realized that it was a plastic bag. It had fallen close to the driver's hand, as if she'd been holding it, and there appeared to be something inside.

Lynch walked over to the car and bent down to get a closer look. When he did, he saw hundreds of small red packets in the melted plastic bag. "Lieutenant," he said quickly. "Come take a look at this."

The lieutenant rushed over and bent down next to Lynch. He poked at the bag and immediately knew what it was. "Looks like a pretty big package of crack."

"I know," Lynch said, looking confused. "I don't think she bought this turning five-dollar tricks in the park."

As Lynch spoke, the crowd that had gathered pressed in for a closer look. When they saw the red-tinged packets, there were gasps that were followed by a single phrase.

"That's Heads shit," someone whispered. Several people repeated the assertion. Then, as if they instinctively knew that it was dangerous to say more, all of them went silent.

It was too late. Lynch had already heard them. "Find out who this Heads is," he said to the lieutenant as he got up. "Because if my hunch is right, this package links this whole thing to Twenty-fifth Street."

"Okay, Captain," the lieutenant said as Lynch walked to his car.

As he got into his vehicle, Lynch's mind drifted to thoughts of Karima, the woman who'd initiated it all. She was determined and vulnerable and all too appealing. He found himself comparing her to his wife.

Just then, his BlackBerry began to vibrate in his pocket. He looked at the number. It was his wife. As the phone continued to vibrate, he thought of all the different ways he could tell her how sorry he was for the way things had turned out that morning. But Kevin Lynch had long ago stopped saying he was sorry, so he did what he always did when faced with such a choice. He pressed IGNORE.

Then he started his car and drove to the meeting that Jansen had helped to arrange at the prison.

As the sun rose against the midmorning sky, the day began to get hotter, and so did the streets. More than at any time in the past few months, there was excitement in the still summer air. Most of it stemmed from the bounty that Heads had placed on Troy.

Heads had spent the morning telling anyone who would listen about the ten-thousand-dollar reward, and bragging about what he would do to the man who'd had the audacity to kill one of his workers. His words were repeated in whispers that floated on the air like butterflies. Each whisper eventually made its way to the bars at 23rd and Cecil B. Moore. Those bars had always been the nerve center of North Philly's streets.

Years before, when Ridge Avenue was Jump Street and Cecil B. Moore Avenue was Columbia, the bars were filled with hustlers in tailored suits and women too delicious for words. In those days, when the aroma of renowned soul food restaurants like Ida's filled the avenue's air, the bars were the places where regular folk and gangsters intermingled. In bars, the laughter was poured into glasses while deals were made and money exchanged. In bars, the Motown Sound gave way to the hopeful, happy songs of Philly International. That generation's hope of a new North Philly died with a single gunshot on a Memphis hotel balcony. Almost instantly, everything changed.

North Philly's hope burned to the ground in riots, and gangs rose up from the smoldering ashes. Six years later, when the single gunshot was replaced by dozens more, a family that had successfully confronted gangs in West Philly brought hope across town with a peace summit called No Gang War in '74. The gangs laid down their arms at 23rd and Ridge that day, and for years there was relative peace.

Nearly thirty years after that summit, 23rd and Ridge was a mere shadow of what it had been. The same bars that had once been the hub of North Philly's nightlife were the starkest reminders of its downfall. The elegance of the old-time hustlers was gone, as was the beauty of the women who'd once joined them in the game. They'd been replaced by drunks who played king for a day with government checks, and women whose beauty had been swallowed up in bottles and crack pipes. When someone from the outside walked in, they were always easy to spot. The response from the bar was always the same: silence.

That's what happened when Skeet, the thirteen-year-old boy who worked with Heads, walked into a bar in search of the man who would help him collect the reward. No one shooed him away. No one questioned his presence. They all simply watched him through the haze of their drunkenness, and waited for the boy to state his business.

They'd all known Skeet since he was old enough to walk. His mother had worked as a barmaid there and had occasionally brought her toddler son to work with her when she had no other choice. After all, leaving her boy at her sister's speakeasy was never an option. She had bigger plans for him, and she spent every waking moment saving and planning for their eventual move to North Carolina, where she hoped to start anew. Somewhere between caring for the drunks and caring for the boy, she stopped looking out for herself.

Two weeks before she and her son were to leave for Raleigh-Durham, two men who'd been casing the bar came in with sawed-off shotguns and shot her during a robbery. She died for the two hundred dollars in the till that day. Since the boy's father was serving a life sentence for murder and his grandparents were all deceased, the aunt she'd tried to keep away from her son was first in line to take the boy and the Social Security check that came with him.

The only thing his aunt ever did for the boy—whose name, like his father's, was Robert Bradley—was to give him the nickname Skeet, because of the way he moved so quickly from one place to another. The actual raising of the boy required more time than she was willing to invest. So she put him in a dirty room on the first floor of her house, gave him a cot, and allowed him to learn from the legions of gamblers and prostitutes who frequented her establishment.

Initially, they saw the boy as a nuisance. As they learned that his mind was sharp enough to grasp the intricacies of the streets, they began to relish the roles of aunts and uncles and old heads and teachers. Soon they were sharing all they knew. By the time he was six, he could identify a straight flush, hustle with loaded dice, and point out the johns who would eventually refuse to pay.

He learned so much at that house that he saw no need for school, where dumbed-down lessons and disinterested teachers had long ago lost his attention. Had his teachers taken just a few moments with him, they would have known, as the hustlers did, that Skeet was mentally gifted. But Skeet was a little black boy, so his playful aggressiveness was pegged as a tendency toward violence. His boredom with the easy lessons was labeled Attention Deficit Disorder. They put him in a class for the learning-disabled and tried to give him medication. Having seen drug dependency close up, he not only refused the medication, he refused to go back to school.

This was his first summer in the only real school he'd ever

known. The lessons he'd learned in the streets were more valuable than anything he'd ever seen in the stuffy brick building with prisonlike metal detectors, and though both schools were grooming him for jail rather than the workforce, the streets at least gave him a chance to survive in either place.

Skeet couldn't remember the days when liquor was the primary business in his aunt's speakeasy, but he remembered that there were old heads who'd seen it all. He'd listened to them tell the stories that had once played out in the crumbling house. Those stories weren't told in the speakeasy anymore. They were told in the bars, and there was one man who told them better than anyone else. That was the man whom Skeet had come to see.

"You know if Mr. Vic here?" Skeet asked the bartender as he took a seat on one of the bar stools.

The bartender wiped a bar glass and looked up with droopy eyes. "He's right over there, Skeet," the bartender said. "Do me a favor. Talk to him outside."

Skeet started to protest, but he knew that the bartender was right. This wasn't the day for a boy to be in a North Philly bar. Not with the cops as hot as they were.

Skeet nodded at the bartender before going over to the table in the corner, where an old man sat hunched over an untouched Jack Daniel's with a Camel cigarette wedged between his lips.

"You got a minute, Mr. Vic?" Skeet asked him as cigarette smoke curled up between them.

Mr. Vic looked at him sideways and coughed mightily. "A minute might be all I got left," he said as he got up from his seat and walked to the door.

Skeet followed him outside, marveling, as he always did, at

Mr. Vic's choice of a regular life over the streets. Skeet had met him years earlier when the old man dated his aunt. He was the closest thing to a father that Skeet had ever known.

He'd often heard stories of Mr. Vic's days as a numbers runner in the 1960s. Back then, he was never without a Cadillac and a woman too young to know better. But when Mr. Vic watched an old friend pay for loose lips with a bullet to the head, Mr. Vic gave up his hustle, though he never gave up the streets.

With unkempt gray hair, a wrinkled black face, and piercing brown eyes, the old man was easy to underestimate. He liked it that way. It allowed him to remain plugged in without being out front.

From his inconspicuous seat in the bar, Mr. Vic had spent years watching things change. Along the way, he'd come to know every new twist on every old game. He'd forgotten more about North Philly than men like Heads would ever know. That was why he was still around at the age of seventy, and why Skeet had spent most of his life hanging on Mr. Vic's every word.

"I guess you here about this mornin'," the old man said when the two of them rounded a corner and turned into an abandoned lot.

"I'm just tryin' to look out for Heads," Skeet said, trying to sound as naïve as a thirteen-year-old should be.

Mr. Vic laughed. "I done told you 'bout tryin' to play me, boy."

"Come on, Mr. Vic—"

"Come on my ass. You don't care about Heads no more than I do. You tryin' to get that ten grand."

Skeet smiled in spite of himself. "All right, old head, you got me."

"Yeah, but you ain't got me," Mr. Vic said as he folded his arms and leaned back against the spray-painted graffiti that marred the lot's walls. "I ain't in this shit."

"Why not?"

Mr. Vic placed a cigarette between his lips. "First of all, word already on the street that they found his shit on some ho that crashed a car out in the park."

"Yeah, but the car was the same one the dude that killed Chuck was drivin'. Heads still gotta find him."

"Don't matter. Heads ain't gon' pay that ten grand, whether somebody help him find the dude or not," the old man said, lighting the cigarette with a self-satisfied smirk.

"Yes he is," Skeet said, more to convince himself than Mr. Vic.

"No he ain't, Skeet," Mr. Vic said as he puffed on the cigarette. "He been runnin' 'round all mornin' talkin' and hopin' for some crackhead to run and tell him who stole his package. If what they say turn out to be right, he *might* give 'em a hundred dollars' worth o' crack, but ain't nobody gettin' no ten grand."

"How you know?" Skeet asked, hoping Mr. Vic would stumble when challenged.

"I seen guys like him before," the old man said as he dropped cigarette ashes onto the ground. "Guys that'll lie to they own mother just to make another ten dollars. Now you can believe that shit he talkin' if you want, but one thing for certain, two things for sure. He ain't bit more givin' out ten grand than the man in the moon. So you might as well get that shit out your head right now."

Skeet knew the old man was right. That was why he'd spent the greater part of the morning trying to figure out a way to limit his boss's options. If Heads wanted information, he would at least show the ten thousand dollars. It would be up to Skeet to pocket it.

There weren't many people in the world Skeet would trust with his plan. Mr. Vic was one of them. Trust didn't get you far in North Philly. Then again, if Skeet's plan worked, he wouldn't be in North Philly for long. He had every intention of starting over someplace else—just like his mother had intended for him to do.

"Suppose I told you I had a way to make him give up the money?" Skeet said, knowing he'd already crossed the line that separated workers from hustlers.

Mr. Vic looked down at the wiry young boy and smiled, knowing that Skeet had seen everything imaginable at the speakeasy. Surely the boy knew the risk that he'd taken by even uttering such words, but Mr. Vic cared about Skeet. He reminded him of himself: cunning enough to plan; wise enough to seek counsel; resourceful enough to make it happen.

Mr. Vic knew what the streets could do to those whose youth made them feel invincible. He knew that Skeet was too smart to be needlessly reckless. Mr. Vic also knew that he couldn't stand by and watch another person he cared about lose his life for nothing.

Skeet was like the grandson Mr. Vic never had. While he wished he could talk the boy out of trying to con Heads at all, he knew that Skeet wouldn't listen. Rather than wasting his breath to try to talk sense into the boy, Mr. Vic resolved to help him do it right.

There were two things Mr. Vic needed to know first. He needed to know if Skeet knew the rules of the game, and he needed to know if Skeet understood what it would take to win. Mr. Vic could get the answer to both with a single question.

"What it take to make a man like Heads do somethin' he don't wanna do?" Mr. Vic asked, taking a final drag on his cigarette and tossing it to the ground.

Skeet smiled. "It's only one thing a man don't never turn down," he said in a tone too wise for his years. "And that's a woman."

4.

arilyn stalked through her front door, still angry at the way Lynch had questioned her about her sister's stabbing at the Criminal Justice Center. Dan Jansen came in behind her, locked the door, and waited for her to explode.

As one of a rotating list of FBI agents assigned to protect the star witness in the upcoming federal trial on City Hall corruption, he'd come to know her fairly well. Their relationship had evolved from one of mutual disdain to one of mutual need. And there was something beyond that, something that Jansen didn't want to admit.

Marilyn tossed her purse onto a chair and wheeled on him with furrowed brow, crossed arms, and heaving breasts. "Why did you tell Lynch that Karima could talk to Bill?" she asked angrily.

"Because it's my job," he said calmly.

"No, *I'm* your job!" she shouted, noting the way his eyes wandered up and down her body.

"It's bad enough I'm going to have to testify against people

I've worked with for years!" she shouted as she sashayed across the room, walking back and forth in spiked heels that made her calves bulge with each step. "I don't need Kevin Lynch looking at me like I'm the one who stabbed my sister!"

"Look, I know you didn't have anything to do with it," Jansen said, trying to calm her. "But maybe Karima knows more than she's letting on. And even if I'm no fan of Kevin Lynch, the mayor's murder joined us at the hip. This is a joint investigation now. So if Lynch asks me to help him track down a killer who's probably connected to this case, then that's what I have to do—no matter where the trail leads."

"So where do you think the two people who hate me the most will lead him?" she asked, waving her arms until a button on her blouse came loose. "What do you think they're going to say?"

She walked toward him and Jansen began to lose control. "It doesn't matter what they say if you had nothing to do with it!" he yelled as he struggled to look into her eyes.

"You're wrong!" Marilyn said, moving closer until she was literally up against him. "It does matter! I've been in politics my whole life. The one thing I've learned is that perception is reality. You're too caught up in your own ego to see that! You're blind! Just like every man I've ever known!"

He looked into her eyes and saw a fire that he wanted to extinguish. In that moment, he began to give up the struggle he'd been mounting for so long, and allowed his eyes to devour the sight he'd been trying to ignore.

"I'm not blind, Marilyn," he said as he looked down at the full breasts that were pressed firmly against him.

The barriers that Jansen had built in his mind were crumbling.

He was no longer an FBI agent, and she was no longer a witness. He was simply a man, and she was a woman. Seeing the weakness in his eyes, Marilyn pressed her advantage.

"You must be blind," she said seductively. "Because if you weren't, you'd see that there's no one in this house but you and I."

For a moment, clarity overtook lust, and Jansen took a step backward. "Look, Marilyn, I can't—"

She moved toward him and put her hand over his mouth. Jansen grabbed at her forearm and made a weak attempt to pull her hand away. After a few seconds, he stopped. Marilyn didn't.

"I'm going to move my hand now," she said as she felt him rising against her. "When I do I want you to tell me exactly what you *can* do, because I'm not interested in hearing about what you can't."

Marilyn felt his breath coming faster as they looked into each other's eyes. When she moved her hand away, he moved closer. So did she. All the lust and longing, all the pressure and tension—all of it poured out between them.

Marilyn slid her hand against his crotch and squeezed him. He pushed his fingers into the soft place beneath her skirt. In minutes, they had stripped down to nothing, and Marilyn was straddling him on the living room floor.

His touch was rough, but Marilyn wanted it that way. She melted as his strong fingers dug into the tender flesh of her hips, pulling her down against him with a strength that made her weak.

She liked it, but she didn't want to. Not this much. She had only wanted to use him, but each time his calloused hands caressed her hips and squeezed the round flesh of her bottom, she was drawn to him by something more than the strength of his grip.

She looked down into his eyes as their bodies slid together and locked into place. He pushed up from the floor, gently moving inside her. Then the gentleness was gone.

Marilyn bucked her hips and rode the stilted rhythm of his thrusts. He moaned in spite of himself and she smiled, her lips curling up like the devil's in the dim light that leaked in between the living room's tightly drawn blinds.

"You wanted this the whole time, didn't you?" she hissed as he moved his palms along her breasts and squeezed them together gently.

"No," he said, panting as he reached into her hair and roughly pulled her face down toward his. "You did."

She licked his lips and rubbed her breasts against his chest. Then she rose up, arched her back, and lifted her face toward the ceiling.

She pressed down and he was deep within her. She pressed again and his body screamed out for him to release all that he'd held in for so long. For months he'd watched her, knowing that he couldn't have her, wishing that he could touch her, longing to simply taste her.

He could feel her all around him now, daring him to pour all those months of desire inside her. She squeezed him tight and then released him. She pulled him deep inside and then pushed him out slowly. She rode him masterfully, giving and taking, slowly then quickly, hard and then softly, until he shouted her name. "Marilyn!"

"Shut up," she hissed, rocking hard against him until his face contorted in twisted ecstasy. "Shut up and handle this."

He shut his eyes tightly and moaned, listening to the sound of her thighs rubbing against his own, the whisper of her breath in the darkness, the high-pitched lilt of her throaty moans.

Then he couldn't stand it anymore. With a primal yell, he lifted her and flipped her onto her back. She threw her legs over his shoulders and allowed him to have everything she could give. He took it with his fingers in every part of her and his tongue on every inch of her.

The two of them clawed at one another in the darkness, each of them breathing in the other's desperation. Their moans became shouts, then pants, then silence.

When they were through, she lay against him, panting softly as she ran her fingers through his blond hair. He lay against her breast and knew that this was wrong. They were on opposite sides of the law, but that was the thing that made it so delicious.

"You should leave," she said while lying against him and swirling his chest hairs around her fingers.

"I can't," he said soberly, sighing at the irony. "I have to protect you."

Marilyn thought back, and remembered the power Jansen had exerted over her. She remembered the look of disdain he'd given her as he revealed in a press conference that city officials had been cooperating with the federal investigation of City Hall. It was the kind of look that an average man wouldn't dare cast in the direction of a woman like the beautiful Marilyn Johnson, who'd risen through the ranks of Philadelphia politics using guile and fear. And yet this man had dared to challenge her, and in doing so, he'd brought her to her knees. He'd been the first man in a long time to do so.

Now the power she'd spent decades trying to build was all but gone. She was down to her basic self—sexual, conniving, selfish. She'd used what she had left to turn the tables on Jansen, and soon she'd use him to turn the tables on them all.

Marilyn got up and walked naked to the front window. She pulled the blinds back slightly and looked out onto her tree-lined street in Philadelphia's affluent Chestnut Hill neighborhood. The trees hissed as they were rustled by a springtime breeze. The single homes and manicured lawns sat quietly, as if they were waiting for something to happen. Everything was as it should be, except for the black Mercury that circled the block and parked thirty yards from Marilyn's home.

"Did you ask for an extra agent to come by the house?" she asked as she watched the car.

Jansen pulled on his pants, scrambled to the window, and looked out. "That's not an agent," he said matter-of-factly. "That's a Philadelphia police detective."

"I imagine Captain Lynch has them watching me," she said, closing the curtain.

"Good thing you don't know anything about what happened to your sister today," Jansen said with a hint of sarcasm as he watched her suspiciously.

She looked at him and smiled. He still didn't trust her. The feeling was mutual. As they dressed in silence, Marilyn began to think of what she could do with Jansen under her control.

She had only one regret. She wished she could have tamed the agent before he had agreed to let her niece talk to her husband.

Karima had held up well through an hour and a half of paperwork at the Philadelphia Industrial Correctional Center. She was fine when they asked questions to double-check her contact information. She was calm when they confiscated her personal effects, including her high-end purse, her money, and her Trio. But when she was strip-searched and saw her mother's blood on her clothes, her grief and guilt collided and she screamed in utter anguish.

The earsplitting sound filled the tiny room with grief. It shook the very walls. The two female guards conducting the search stepped away—not because they couldn't subdue her, but because they knew what Karima had endured.

They watched as the naked young woman slumped to the floor and held the bloody clothes, hugging them like she wished she could hug her mother. They saw her cry uncontrollably as her emotions, like her body, lay uncovered on the cold concrete.

They felt sympathy as they witnessed Karima pull her knees to her chest and curl up in a ball, rocking back and forth as she looked toward the heavens accusingly. "Why?" Karima yelled as she clutched the bloody clothes. "Why do you hurt everyone I love?"

The guards looked at each other and then at Karima. One of them tried to quiet her. "Calm down, honey," she said, moving closer and placing a hand on Karima's shoulder.

Karima jerked away and released a grief-filled shriek, angrily ripping the bloodstained pants in half.

"Why?" she screamed, looking up as the guards looked on. "You took the only man I ever loved! You took my father away before I could even know him! You made my mother hate herself and snatched her the minute she loved me! Why, God? Why!"

Four more female guards came into the room. One of them carried a blanket. The other three carried their clubs. Karima backed into the corner, her teeth bared and her fists clenched as the guards began closing in.

For a moment, she considered fighting them. Then the pain of all she had suffered over the past year crashed down, and her will to fight was sapped. From the six-month prison stint she'd served to protect Duane, to being accused of murdering the mayor, to watching the man she loved die in front of her, she'd seen far too much. Being stripped to nothing but her emotions and her mother's blood had broken her.

Karima dropped the bloody pants and sank to the floor, weeping quietly. She stayed there for what seemed an eternity, crying all the tears she'd held in for so long.

"I'm sorry," she said as the guards gently covered her with a blanket and helped her to her feet. "This is all my fault—all of it."

As they led her out of the room, she repeated those words again and again. They thought she was apologizing for her outburst. She wasn't. Karima was apologizing for all the lives she believed she had wrecked—beginning with her own.

Thirty minutes passed and the tears had come and gone. Now there was only the reality of the moment: a cell, an orange jumpsuit, and a determination to find out who had stabbed her mother.

Karima looked up as footsteps moved toward her cell. "Thomas," a female guard said as she unlocked the door. "Come with us."

Two guards escorted Karima down a long hallway and ushered her through several locked gates.

The one with the keys opened a door and indicated that Karima should walk through it alone. Hesitantly, she did. When the door closed behind her, a familiar voice spoke from the other side of the room.

"Hello, Karima," Lynch said. He was sitting down at a table in the dimly lit room with Karima's lawyer beside him. "I need to ask you a few questions."

"Not before I ask mine," she said, standing near the door and wringing her hands nervously.

"If it's about your mother," Lynch said, as Karima's lawyer looked on, "she's alive. I spoke to the doctors at Hahnemann right before I got here. She's in critical condition, but it looks like the ice pick missed her spinal cord and didn't make it to her brain. She's still unconscious and under heavy sedation."

Karima sat down in a heap, the weight of the world seemingly lifting from her shoulders as she digested the news. "Is she going to make it?"

"The doctors aren't sure," Lynch said.

Karima clenched and unclenched her fists. There would be no more tears at that moment, no more blaming God for what had happened. Now there was only the business of avenging her mother. That was all that mattered to Karima.

"So what do you know so far?" she asked, turning to Lynch.

"There's a good chance the same man who stabbed your mother stabbed a guy who worked for a drug dealer named Heads in North Philly. We've got Heads's corner staked out now, but other than that—"

"You've got nothing," she said, completing the sentence. "So what do you want from me?"

"I want anything you know that can help us catch the man who did this," Lynch said matter-of-factly.

"And you?" Karima asked, looking at her lawyer. "What are you doing here? You're supposed to be working on getting me out."

"We need a hundred thousand to make ten percent of the bail. The only thing you have worth that is your mother's house. Without her permission to sign it over, there's nothing I can do. Unless . . ."

He looked at Lynch expectantly.

"Unless what?" Her eyes darted back and forth between them.

"Unless you can get someone else to put up the money," Lynch said.

"Someone like who?" Karima said, her tone impatient.

The door behind her opened and a fiftysomething man in shackles was led into the room by two federal marshals. He was tall and handsome, just as she remembered him, with silver hair and eyes like shining black marbles. His mustache and beard were trimmed for the occasion, and his eyes were bright with a mix of anticipation and nerves.

The marshals sat him down in the seat beside Karima, then stood aside and watched the man who was now in federal custody for his role in the murder of Mayor Tatum.

Karima looked at him, unsure of what to say, uncertain of what to call him, uncomfortable with the knowledge she'd learned about him just two months before. She was happy to see him, though. Just a half hour ago, she'd been asking God why he'd been taken away.

"How about starting with hello?" Lynch said in a weak attempt to break the ice.

Bill Johnson smiled. Karima couldn't. The man beside her was the only man her mother had ever loved, and because he was married to Marilyn, her mother could never have him. The only thing of his that Sharon had was Karima. Now it seemed that the only thing Karima might have left of her mother was him.

"Hello, Karima," he said plaintively. "It's good to see you."

"Is it really?" Karima asked coldly. "I don't know if I can say the same. Especially under these circumstances."

Lynch could see the anger in her eyes as she spoke. There was something magnetic about it. He stared at her for a moment before her father interrupted his thoughts.

"I wish we had the privacy to talk about all the things we need to," Bill Johnson said, his voice filled with regret.

"Privacy?" Karima said, exasperated. "For what? Everyone knows you slept with my mother while you were married to my aunt, and everyone knows you're my father. I just want to know why you never told me."

"I couldn't."

"Why?"

"Look, Karima, I don't want to get into this now."

"I've waited twenty-three years for an answer," Karima said angrily. "So I don't think *now* is an unreasonable time to get it."

The other men in the room looked on as Bill Johnson struggled to find a response worth giving. When he spoke, it was with a clarity that no one in the room expected.

"I loved your mother," he said quietly. "But when I told Marilyn I wanted a divorce, she just laughed. You see, she knew things about my family. Terrible things she threatened to expose if I ever left her."

Lynch looked at Bill Johnson with a measure of sympathy, and hoped that what he was about to say would impact the case at hand.

"My mother was soft, beautiful, and fragile," Bill said with a faraway look. "My father was huge. He had a big heart. He had great intellect. And he was fiercely protective. He was everything a man should be. In the early sixties, for a black man in Philadelphia, all that got you was trouble. My father didn't want that. He just wanted a way to take care of his family."

Bill looked at Karima. "He asked your grandfather to help him to get a job with the city."

Karima nodded at the mention of her grandfather, the first black state senator in Pennsylvania.

"My father took me to the senator's house," Bill said. "That's when I met your mother and Marilyn for the first time. We were just kids, playing in the den while my father talked to your grandfather, but even then I could see the difference between them: Marilyn was saucy, and your mother was sweet."

Bill's eyes glazed over for a moment. He looked like he was caught in the past. Karima seemed to be caught there, too.

"My father worked his way up to supervisor in the office of the Clerk of Quarter Sessions," Bill said. "He was responsible for keeping court records. It was a good job—enough for my mom to stay home and take care of me and Dad.

"When I was about seven, things started to change. Whenever spring came, my mother's face would get full and she'd stay in her room. By summer she would be back to normal. She'd come out and laugh and talk. Things seemed okay.

"They weren't, though. Every once in a while, I would see my mother upstairs crying and begging God to forgive her. I used to ask her what was wrong, but she would never tell me. She would never tell *anyone*.

"Then one day—I must have been about ten—I was playing in the backyard, digging for buried treasure or something. My shovel hit something hard and hollow. I brushed away the dirt and saw that it was a wooden box. I dug around it and found two more. When I opened them there were tiny bones inside. Bones of the babies my mother had smothered right after they were born."

Tears welled up in Bill's eyes, but he wouldn't allow them to fall. "I told my father what I'd found and he wasn't surprised. See, he had helped her cover it up. Turns out I was the only child they kept. My mother didn't want us to have to struggle financially to feed and clothe more children. So she just . . . got rid of them. I guess she loved having money more than she loved those babies, and I guess my father loved her enough not to say anything. Both of them suffered for it, though. They never got over what they did."

The room was silent. Karima was the first to break it. "So how did Marilyn find out?"

Bill placed his shackled hands on the table and looked down at them. "My father couldn't be sure if I would keep the secret. So that night, he dug up the boxes and took them down to an incinerator in South Philly. A night watchman saw him and threatened to call the police. My father called your grandfather and the senator made the whole thing go away. Your grandfather kept a journal of those types of favors—just in case someone got out of line. When he died, he left a will. Marilyn inherited some of his money, but more importantly, he left her the contents of his safe-deposit box. The only thing inside the box was the journal. He thought she would know what to do with it, and it turned out he was right."

Bill laughed bitterly. "For years, Marilyn used the secrets in that journal to twist arms and rise through the political ranks. With what she knew, she could control everyone around her—including me."

He turned and stared into Karima's eyes. "I loved your mother, Karima. I still do. But I couldn't risk Marilyn digging up the past and sending my mother to jail. So I did what Marilyn wanted: I stayed with her and kept my mouth shut about you. If I had talked, Marilyn would've destroyed my whole family—even you. I thought I owed it to you to protect you from that."

Bill sighed, releasing decades of hurt as he looked into Karima's eyes. "My parents passed a few years ago—just months apart. Looking back on it now, I guess I passed away, too. I passed the day I realized that I would never have the chance to be your father."

Karima saw herself in his eyes, though she couldn't bring herself to forgive him yet.

"Never say never," she said, almost in a whisper. "There's always another chance."

Bill Johnson's eyes softened along with his daughter's heart. "That's what I've come to give you," he said. "Another chance."

Karima looked confused. "What do you mean?"

"He means he's here to set you free," her lawyer said, glancing at Bill Johnson. "Apparently from more than just this prison."

"I don't see how," Karima said, looking from her lawyer to her father for an explanation. It was Lynch who provided it.

"Earlier, you told me that if I knew anything at all about you, I'd know you wouldn't stop until you found the truth about your mother's stabbing," Lynch said to Karima. "Well, I think you're right. Your father's lawyer has power of attorney over some of his assets. He's arranged to post bail. You'll be my responsibility when you're released, and you'll be out of here in an hour."

Karima turned to Bill Johnson, and for the first time in her life, she said words she never believed she'd be able to say. "Thank you . . . Dad."

The tears that had welled up in his eyes toppled over the edges and rolled slowly down his cheeks. "You're welcome, baby."

The two lifted their shackled hands and touched each other's fingertips. The marshals in the back of the room edged closer, but Bill and Karima ignored them as they touched away the years of hurt.

"Come on, Mr. Johnson," one of the marshals said, tapping his shoulder. "We've got to get you back to the Federal Detention Center."

"One question before you take him," Lynch said quickly.

Bill Johnson looked at Lynch expectantly.

"The journal Marilyn has—the one with her father's list of people he did favors. Do you know where she keeps it?"

"She never told me," Bill said as he rose to leave with the federal marshals. "I suspect it's somewhere in our house. There are lots of things hidden in our house."

It took only twenty minutes for Troy to drive the old man's van from Fairmount Park to the northwest section of the city using the curve-filled drives where almost no one took their eyes off the road to look at other drivers.

With the old man's body laid out behind the driver's seat, and his blood soaking down into the carpet, Troy knew that he would have to switch vehicles. But he knew he had other business to attend to first.

He parked the van at an apartment complex near Lincoln Drive and turned off the engine. Then he got out of the driver's seat and looked down at the old man's body before turning him over and removing his wallet from his back pocket. He took out the driver's license to make sure the address was still the same. Then he took the man's keys and walked the half block to the house he remembered from his youth.

He'd been watching the house for the past month, and he knew that Mrs. Williams still worked as a housekeeper at Albert Einstein Medical Center. She normally returned from her work on the night shift at 9:00 A.M. So he expected that she would be home now, since it was a little after eleven.

He tried three keys before he got to the one that opened the front door. He slowly closed the door behind him and walked inside. When he did, it was like he'd stepped back in time. The mingled odors of Lysol and Spic and Span were thick in the air, and the pictures on the walls leading to the living room were faded. His memories, however, were fresh in his mind.

As he walked into the house, he heard the sound of Mrs. Williams's laughter from fourteen years before, and in the dark recesses of his troubled mind, Troy was nine years old once again.

He'd walked home from school the day Mrs. Williams had damaged him. He was smiling as he walked in the door, reading the note he'd gotten from a girl in his class.

Mrs. Williams was waiting at the door when he walked in.

"What's that?" she asked, snatching the note from his hands.

"Give it back," he pleaded. "It's private!"

"Private?" she snapped. "You ain't got nothin' private. This my house!"

Troy reached up in an attempt to get the note back from her, but Mrs. Williams smiled wickedly and held it high above her head. He tried to grab it again and she smacked his face, sending him sprawling across the floor.

"You don't try to snatch nothin' from me," she said as she opened the folded sheet of paper and read it silently.

Chuck, her other foster child, came home from school at that moment, and saw Troy weeping near the door. When he looked up and saw Mrs. Williams standing a few feet away, he knew that she was the cause of Troy's tears.

Mrs. Williams began to chuckle while Chuck looked on. Within seconds, her chuckle had grown to full-blown laughter.

"Why you laughin', Miss Williams?" Chuck asked as his face creased in a half-smile.

She read the note aloud in a singsong, teasing voice. "'Troy,'" she said, sounding like a schoolgirl, "'will you be my boyfriend?'"

Both she and Chuck laughed loudly as Troy cowered in humiliation.

"You more girl than she is! How you gon' be somebody's boyfriend?" Mrs. Williams asked as she and Chuck exploded in laughter.

Normally, Troy withered under the weight of their scorn. This time, he tried to stand up to them.

"I'm not a girl," he said softly.

Mrs. Williams stopped laughing abruptly. "What did you say?"

Troy sat up from the floor and found his voice. "I'm not a girl," he said more aggressively.

She flew over to him, snatched him up, and marched him to the hall closet. As Troy struggled to get away from her, she pulled a housedress from the closet and forced it over his head.

"If I say you a girl," she said as she punched and smacked him in his face, "you a girl!"

Chuck laughed uproariously as Troy fell to the floor with blood on his face and tears in his eyes.

That was the last time he'd stood up to her, and the last time he'd been certain of who he was.

Now, as he walked into the house where his childhood had been taken, the memories fueled the anger he brought with him.

The threadbare brown carpet looked just like it did on that day fourteen years before. It muffled his footsteps as he walked into the vestibule and drew out his ice pick. He moved carefully, watching and listening as he padded down the hall toward the living room. He was just a few feet away when a board squeaked beneath his feet. He stopped and waited, listening for the sound of Mrs. Williams moving toward him.

As he stood there, he heard the sound of a television. A reporter spoke in troubled tones as he recounted the events of the morning. "We now have footage of the man police are seeking in connection with the early-morning stabbing of Sharon Thomas in a Center City courtroom," he said. "Sharon Thomas is the mother of Karima Thomas, whose preliminary hearing in connection with the murder of Mayor Jeffrey Tatum led to the judge's decision to hold her over for trial on attempted murder, assault, and weapons charges. According to police, Karima Thomas is being held on one million dollars' bail. No word yet on whether she will be able to make bail and secure her release."

Troy took three large steps and peered around the wall to survey the living room. There was a sofa and love seat encased in plastic slipcovers, and there was an easy chair facing the television. He could see Mrs. Williams's head as she sat in the chair.

Troy moved slowly as he crept up behind her. With each step he took, he thought of the beatings he'd endured at her hands. He thought of the way she'd berated him as a child. He thought of the years of anger that he'd harbored. When he was directly behind the chair, he thought of how much pleasure he'd take in killing her.

Troy looked down at the sleeping old woman, twisted his mouth into a maniacal grin, raised his ice pick high above his head, and prepared to plunge it deep into her chest. He wanted her to sense his presence first. He wanted her to turn around, to open her mouth to scream. But there was nothing.

Mrs. Williams didn't move for a full ten seconds. Troy reached down and poked her shoulder with his hand. She tipped over and tumbled out of the chair, since she'd died about an hour before of a heart attack.

Enraged, he fell to his knees in front of her and plunged the ice pick into her cold, dead flesh. "I'm not a girl!" he shouted as he stabbed her again. "I'm a man! A man!"

He shouted those words a dozen times as he stabbed her in her face and chest. When he was finished, he fell over her body and grieved for everything she'd taken from him.

For a while, all he heard was the sound of his own anguish. Then the sound of the television penetrated his madness.

"The man in this footage is wanted in connection with the courtroom stabbing of Sharon Thomas," the reporter said, looking down at a notepad as the images of Troy in the courtroom played repeatedly. "Police are asking that anyone who sees him or can provide a name for this man call 911 immediately. We are getting unconfirmed reports that there may be another victim in North Philadelphia who may have been attacked and killed by the same man."

Troy took one last look at Mrs. Williams. "You and Chuck won't be laughing anymore," he said before spitting in her face.

A second later, he stood up and took his list from his back pocket. He crossed off number four and ran upstairs to the bathroom. Stripping quickly, he got into the shower and washed the blood from his face and hands.

He went into the bedroom and found a pair of reading glasses on the dresser. Then he rummaged through Mr. Williams's closet and found a set of ill-fitting green work clothes, a tight baseball cap, and boots a size too large. He looked in the back of the closet for the toolbox he remembered from his youth. He found it beneath a pile of clothes.

Quickly he opened it, and removed two trays of tools to get to the treasure on the bottom. He smiled when he saw the same .38 snub-nosed revolver that he and Chuck had found once when they were playing years ago. Troy had often fantasized about using that gun to kill the Williamses, though he'd never had the heart to go through with it.

Now the Williamses were dead. But there was much more to

be done. The gun would come in handy. Troy pulled on the old man's work clothes before running down the stairs and into the living room to get the keys to Mrs. Williams's car.

He was on his way out the back door when he heard a piece of news that stopped him in his tracks.

"And this just in," the reporter said excitedly. "A spokesman for the Philadelphia Prisons has just confirmed that Karima Thomas will be released on bail within the hour. We have no further details, but stay tuned to News Ten for the latest updates on this fast-developing story. This is Harold Mays, News Ten, reporting live from the Criminal Justice Center in Philadelphia."

Troy smiled as he sauntered out the back door and started Mrs. Williams's car.

He knew he'd meet Karima soon enough. But he had pressing business to attend to first.

5.

Skeet sat in the room he'd slept in since he was four, looking at the peeling paint that adorned the walls, and the moldy bedsheets that covered the room's only window. He'd never bothered to change much about his corner of his aunt's three-story speakeasy, preferring to sleep in a place he knew rather than a place he liked. Besides, if he changed it, he'd no longer have a reason to leave, and Skeet wanted desperately to leave.

For nine years he'd felt the dampness in the air from a basement that flooded every time it rained. He'd listened to the sounds of prostitutes arguing with customers, and the heavy footfall of drunks stumbling in the hall. He'd felt the cold stares of gamblers who played poker with guns on the table, and he'd seen more than one body in the alley beside his window.

Skeet had long ago grown tired of the hopelessness of this place. He hated the way it beat people into submission. He hated the tired looks on everyone's faces. He hated the men who refused to take jobs, but worked like dogs for five dollars' worth of crack. He hated the stench of unwashed women whose cycles seemed never to end. The house was like one of those women. It was conniving. It was filthy, and the blood never seemed to stop flowing.

Skeet was ready to move on, but he knew that moving on would take a plan. That was why he and Mr. Vic had come back to the house after talking at the bar. Taking out Heads was merely a matter of outthinking him. The question was what they would do afterward.

Skeet looked at the old man, examined the wrinkles in his jet-black skin, and tried to figure out just what he was thinking. Mr. Vic didn't return the look, so Skeet figured he wasn't ready to talk. While he waited, he turned on the black-and-white, battery-operated television he kept next to his bed.

When the picture came into focus, Skeet found himself staring into the face of the man who'd stabbed Chuck.

"The big story on Action News is the courtroom stabbing of Sharon Thomas, mother of Karima Thomas, whose preliminary hearing resulted in her being held over for trial on charges stemming from Mayor Tatum's murder. Police are seeking this man, as yet unidentified, in connection with the Sharon Thomas stabbing and another stabbing in North Philadelphia."

As the reporter spoke, Mr. Vic joined Skeet in front of the small screen and watched as the killer's picture appeared again and again. As they watched the blurry images from the courtroom, they were certain of only one thing: they'd never seen him before.

"Everybody in North Philly gon' tell Heads they know him," Skeet said, his voice laced with frustration. "How we gon' get the money when they got his picture on the news?"

"That ain't what I'm worried about," Mr. Vic said, his tone as uncertain as his words.

"What you worried about, then?"

Mr. Vic didn't answer. Instead, he thought about the bond between him and the boy. They were attached in a way that Mr. Vic and Skeet's aunt had never been. While the young boy with his backward cap and low-slung jeans looked different from the old man wearing spit-shined shoes and a fedora, the two were alike in many ways, especially in their willingness to do for one another.

Mr. Vic had spent years doing his best to show the boy something other than the filth that was paraded in front of him every day. He'd taken him to his first and only basketball game. He'd shown him how to change the brake pads on a Cadillac. He'd given him a glimpse of the other side of manhood. During those times, Skeet had grown to love and admire Mr. Vic. And though he had never admitted it, the old man loved him, too.

Therein lay the dilemma. If he helped the boy get the money from Heads and something went wrong, Skeet's blood would be on his hands. As hard a man as he had once been, Mr. Vic wasn't sure if he could ever forgive himself for that.

"Skeet, I been thinkin'," he said, as the news report went from courtroom pictures to old footage of Karima Thomas in handcuffs.

" 'Bout what?" Skeet mumbled, though he was paying more attention to the images on the screen than to Mr. Vic.

The old man got up, walked over to the window, and pulled back the dirty sheet that covered it.

"I been thinkin' 'bout you," Mr. Vic said as he looked out at the trash-strewn alley.

Skeet looked up at him expectantly, waiting for Mr. Vic to tell him a truth he'd never heard before.

"I been watchin' you since you was four," the old man said, his tone wistful. "I always knew you was smarter than these dumb-asses around here. I guess that's why I tried to help you whenever I could. But I was in the game a long time, Skeet, and even though it's a lot more people in it now, ain't nothin' 'bout the game changed. People hearts still the same. They just got guns to make it easier to do what they want to do."

Mr. Vic sighed. "I watched my friend take a bullet 'cause he ran his mouth to this woman he was tryin' to lay down with. He figured he could get her if he told her the cats we worked for wasn't shit. He told her he was the real gangster. Said he could take 'em out whenever he wanted to. Course he was just bullshittin', but she ain't know that.

"Couple days later, she went and told somebody what he said. When word got back, they shot him dead in the street, right there on Columbia Avenue."

Skeet sat silently for a few moments. Then, with furrowed brow, he asked the only question he could. "What that got to do with me?"

The old man turned from the window. "Same way you talkin' now—like you just gon' take down your boss—that's how he was talkin' then. He died for it. You willin' to die, too?"

Skeet looked up at the exposed wood slats under the punctured and water-stained plaster on the ceiling. He looked across the room at the holes in the woodwork where mice shuttled in and out. He took a deep breath and caught the ever-present stench of sweat and urine before exhaling in frustration.

"You don't think I'm dead now, Mr. Vic?" he asked as his eyes filled with tears that he refused to let fall. "Looka this room, man. Looka this house. Looka these people. You think bein' stuck in here better than bein' dead? I rather take my chances with a bullet than live like this, man. 'Cause at least with a bullet I ain't just sittin' here waitin' for this shit to swallow me up."

"I know what it's like, son."

"No, you don't!" Skeet said, raising his voice for the first time. "You don't know what it's like when everybody think you gon' end up dead or in jail. When your own aunt don't care what happen to you."

"That ain't true, Skeet, she—"

"She a drunk, Mr. Vic! She in there laid out on the bed right now, pissy drunk. That's why *you* don't fuck with her no more. So if my own peoples don't care what happen to me, and don't nobody else care what happen to me—"

"I care!" the old man shouted, and silence dropped like a curtain between them.

Neither of them knew what to say next. They lived in a world where men didn't say those types of things to one another. Not fathers to sons. Not friends to friends. Not brothers to brothers. Both of them were entering into something new. As the eldest of the two, Mr. Vic decided to test the waters first.

"I always wanted to tell you that, Skeet," he said, looking down in embarrassment. "It just wasn't never the right time."

"Mr. Vic, I—"

"Skeet, you ain't gotta say nothin'. Whatever you got to say I already know anyway. I just need you to know I understand what you goin' through. God knows I wish I coulda took you outta here and put you someplace decent, but your aunt wouldn't let that happen, 'cause she get that check for you. Maybe this thing with Heads is your way out, and maybe you should take it."

The old man folded his hands and looked down at them for half a minute as the television droned on in the background, showing the same pictures repeatedly.

"I am gon' take it, Mr. Vic," Skeet said, once again staring at the television screen. "I just gotta find out who this dude is."

Mr. Vic smiled. "No, you don't," he said. "You gotta use what you already know about Heads to bring him down. What's his weakness?"

Skeet was quiet for a moment. There were so many weaknesses that none of them immediately came to the surface, but underneath them all was one glaring flaw.

"He wanna be bigger than he is," Skeet said quietly. "Like Duane Faison used to be."

"Then you play on that, and get somethin' else to throw in with it. You gotta go back to that house and learn somethin' 'bout this killer that nobody else know."

"Why? So I can find him?"

"I ain't say nothin' 'bout findin' him."

"But I thought—"

"I ain't say nothin' 'bout thinkin', either," Mr. Vic said firmly. "I said learn."

Duly chastised, Skeet sat back and waited for further instructions.

"Everybody already know the package burned up in that car fire, but don't nobody know nothin' 'bout the dude that took it. Heads still gotta find out who he is, where he came from, who he know, and where to find him," Mr. Vic said, his words coming faster as the plan came together in his mind. "Course the cops gon' know half o' that 'fore you even get a chance to talk to Heads, so you gotta act like you knew it first. That mean whatever you find out, you add two or three little things that make it sound better."

"What if Heads ask me how I know?"

"Just tell him it's word on the street. He don't need to know more than that. You want him to be countin' on you for all his information at first. Then when he press you, you pass him off to a woman to close the deal."

"I just wish it was more than ten grand," Skeet said, almost to himself.

"It *is* gon' be more than ten grand," the old man said with a smile. "By the time you finish with him, you gon' have it all."

"Yeah, but what you gon' have, Mr. Vic?"

The old man smiled. "If you throw me a couple dollars I'll take it, but what I really want from you is a promise."

"What kinda promise?"

"I want you to leave North Philly and never come back. Not for me. Not for nobody."

Skeet didn't know if he could leave the old man behind. Now that he had one person in the world who cared about him, he wasn't sure if he wanted to let him go, so he made the promise, even though he knew it was false.

"I promise I won't come back," he said, looking the old man in the eye. "Not that it make much difference. We gotta get the money first."

"No," Mr. Vic said. "We gotta get the facts first. Once we get that, I'll send you the woman that'll bring him down. One that's fine, smart, and willin' to risk it all."

Karima Thomas stepped out into the midafternoon sunshine and stood at the prison's gate flanked by Lynch and her lawyer, holding nothing more than her clutch containing a Trio and forty dollars.

Her lawyer had gone to her mother's house and brought back a pair of jeans and a white cotton blouse so she could avoid putting on her bloodstained clothes. He'd brought her a pair of sensible espadrilles so she could walk quickly to the car. He'd also brought his lawyerly answers so she could avoid the invasive questions that were sure to come.

Lynch had much more than that. He'd brought feelings, the kind that wouldn't allow him to let a murderer walk free any longer than he had to. He'd seen enough death and destruction during his years in Homicide—from the death of a little girl in The Bridge to the death of a sitting mayor. If there was one thing he'd learned from experience, it was that the people closest to the victims always knew more than he did.

That was why he'd sent detectives to Marilyn's home and requested a warrant to search for the journal Bill had told them about. It was why he was willing to bring Karima to the table. At least, that's what he told himself. Deep down, he knew there were other reasons that he'd never share with anyone—not even himself. He knew that she would bring an unrelenting zeal to the investigation. He knew that she would bring a sharp intelligence as well. Still, he didn't know how he would control her tendency toward ruthlessness. In truth, he wasn't sure that he wanted to.

"You ready?" Lynch asked her as he looked out at the dozens of news vehicles lined up along State Road with their cameras trained on Karima.

"Yes," she said.

Lynch began to move toward the gate.

"Wait," she said, grabbing his arm and looking up at him with eyes at once determined and vulnerable.

He stopped.

"Thank you," she said softly.

"I didn't do it just for you," Lynch said, sounding almost defensive.

"I know, but it feels like you did," she said with a sigh. "I guess when you've lost as much as I have, you grab on to anything that looks like kindness, and hold on for dear life."

"Well, if I'm the only one showing you kindness, that means you owe me," Lynch said with a chuckle.

Karima smiled, but there was fire in her eyes. "I think I owe a lot of people."

"I hope you're not planning to pay them all back," Lynch said with a warning in his voice.

Karima paused. "I'm planning to do what I always do when I'm pushed," she said. "I'm planning to do the right thing."

Karima's lawyer watched Lynch's eyes shift back and forth, searching for an appropriate response. It looked as if Lynch were breathless. Karima noticed it, too. The lawyer interrupted before the moment could stretch out any longer.

"Let's go," the lawyer said, nodding at the guard who controlled the gate.

When it opened, a five-officer police detail from the Dignitary Protection Unit surrounded them. Then hundreds of curious onlookers joined with scores of reporters to surge toward the gate.

They blocked a van filled with incoming prisoners that had been moving toward a separate entrance. They moved past the sheriff's deputies who'd been called in to assist correctional officers with crowd control. As the crowd pushed harder to get closer to Karima, the deputies and COs who normally handled prisoners used their heavy-handed tactics on civilians.

Several skirmishes broke out. Traffic on nearby State Road came to a halt as motorists stopped to observe the commotion. Karima, Lynch, and the lawyer, surrounded by the five-member police squad, continued to move through the crowd toward a waiting car.

Shouted questions rained down on them as cameramen and photographers grappled with officers and one another to get the best shot. Reporters' voices shouted questions that Karima couldn't hear. Curious onlookers surged through the contingent of prison personnel and sheriff's deputies until they were just a few feet from Karima. The lawyer held his briefcase in front of him and pushed their police escort forward. Lynch placed his arm around Karima's shoulder to protect her from the onslaught. Just as they prepared to get into the car, a single voice rang out over the commotion.

"Kevin!" It was a high-pitched, frantic tone that made him stop in his tracks.

Instinctively, Lynch snatched his arm from Karima's shoulder and looked around in the crowd. It didn't take him long to spot her.

Curled reddish-brown dreadlocks dropped down to her shoulders. Her eyes were brown, too, and large enough to hold the joy and pain of seventeen years. Her skin was smooth and supple in ways that Lynch hadn't noticed when they'd argued that morning. Her beauty was that of a woman who'd raised a man and a child all at once.

"Get in the car," Lynch said to Karima and the lawyer. "I'll be there in a minute."

They did as he asked, but not before following his eyes as he looked through the crowd. Karima spotted her first. The two women locked eyes for a moment before Karima cast a troubled look in Lynch's direction and got into the car.

Lynch closed the car door and stalked through the crowd, pushing people and reporters aside. "This isn't a good time, Jocelyn," he said to his wife in a tone that barely concealed his annoyance.

She looked at the car. "I can see that. Looks like Ms. Thomas is keeping you busy."

Lynch sighed impatiently. "Look, honey, I promise I'll be home tonight. We can talk then."

"Don't make those kinds of promises, Kevin," his wife said, speaking gently in spite of her anger. "You know you can't keep them."

"Yes I can. I—"

"You promised our daughter you'd take her to Penn to look at the dorms today," his wife said evenly. "She's still waiting."

Lynch tried to think of something that would make it all right, though he knew nothing would. Too many times his work had gotten in the way of his family, and more than once, his work had involved women too beautiful to ignore. Jocelyn had questioned him about it only once, when he'd gone back to The Bridge to help his childhood friend find her lost child. Now she was beyond questions. She just wanted answers.

"I'm sorry," Lynch said, looking anxiously toward the car before turning his attention to his wife.

Jocelyn's eyes took on a sadness that said everything and nothing at all. "You know, Kevin, I used to think we'd get to some moment in our lives that was special enough to make you want to share it. Or that I'd look good enough to make you want to come home at night. Or that these last seventeen years were special enough to make you want to put our family first. I've stopped thinking like that."

"Jocelyn, I said I'm sorry," he said, growing tense.

"I know, Kevin," she said sadly. "I'm sorry, too."

The crowd noise grew louder as the police began to push people away from the car containing Karima and her lawyer. Lynch turned around to make sure everything was okay. Then he turned around to speak to his wife, but she was already walking away.

He watched her for a moment, admiring the way her body had matured. Her hips were still round, her bottom still firm, and she moved with a sensuality that was natural, not forced. He'd appreciated that once. Somewhere deep down, he still did. It just didn't excite him anymore.

"Captain Lynch!" the lawyer called out from the car.

Lynch ran over to them and got in the front seat with the driver. "What is it?" he said, turning around.

The lawyer mumbled something into his cell phone, then disconnected the call. "I just got off the phone with the hospital," he said, closing his cell phone. "Sharon Thomas just woke up. She's in critical condition, and they don't know how long she'll be lucid."

Lynch looked over at the driver. "Get us down to Hahnemann Hospital. Now!"

The concierge was in his twenties, a dark-haired young man from nearby Camden, New Jersey. He was working his way through Rutgers with a desk job at Cherry Hill's Washington Commons Condominiums. He'd been there for five months, and though he wasn't as experienced as he could have been, the job was fairly easy. He smiled at the residents and helped them with their bags. He signed in the occasional guest, did his homework on his laptop, and when there was a problem, he relied on Renaldo, the maintenance chief, to solve it.

Today, Renaldo wasn't in. He'd left early after receiving a call telling him that his pregnant wife had been hospitalized and was expected to deliver within the hour. The concierge would be alone for the remainder of his shift, but he was confident that he could handle whatever happened until his shift ended at five.

He'd been sitting for half an hour, working on some calculus problems. The place was quiet enough for him to do so around one o'clock. The younger residents who made up the majority of the condo owners were at work, and the retired residents were either out enjoying the summer day in South Jersey or vacationing abroad.

He'd run into a particularly difficult calculus problem when a tall, light-skinned black man in green work clothes came walking through the sliding glass doors carrying a toolbox and a clipboard.

The young concierge closed his laptop and smiled, happy to be able to handle something on his own.

"How you doin'?" the workman said in a soft Southern drawl, pulling a baseball cap over his eyes as he looked down at his clipboard. "I got a call about a leak that might be coming from 6B. Goodman, I believe, just bought the unit."

The concierge thought for a minute. "Are you sure? I don't think anything's on in that unit. It hasn't been touched in a couple of months."

"Well, I got a call this mornin'," the workman said, and his whole face seemed to light up behind the thick black plastic frames of the reading glasses that covered nearly the whole top half of his face. "Guy named Renaldo Vasquez said they just turned the water on and it started leakin', but . . ."

"Oh, *Renaldo* called you," the concierge said, smiling as recognition swept across his face.

"Yeah, he said he was tryin' to get to it, but with his wife havin' a baby and all . . ."

"No problem," the concierge said. "I guess I can take you up and stay with you while you check it out."

"Should only take about ten minutes—fifteen if there's a problem," the workman said as he picked his toolbox up from the floor.

The concierge put a small plastic sign up on the black marble desk that told visitors he'd be back in a moment. Then he escorted the workman up on the elevator.

Once they were inside, the workman went straight to the sink and opened the cabinets below. He reached into his toolbox for a flashlight and bent down on hands and knees as he directed the beam into the cabinet.

"It's a good thing you came," the concierge said, speaking loudly so the workman could hear him from beneath the sink. "The Goodmans were going to have a crew in to do renovations next week and that leak could have really caused some damage."

The workman turned onto his back, the entire top half of his body invisible inside the cabinet. He reached out with one hand. "Can you hand me my monkey wrench?"

The concierge bent down and looked through the contents of the toolbox. "I'm not really good with tools," he said, sounding embarrassed. "Is the monkey wrench the big metal thing with the U-shaped hook on the end?"

"That's it," the workman said.

The concierge handed it to him. There was the sound of grunting and metal banging against metal as the workman fiddled with something beneath the sink. It took him a few minutes, but eventually he began to work his way out from the cabinet. He stood up with the monkey wrench in his hand.

"So, how bad is it?" the concierge said.

"Looks like it's gonna be fine," the workman said with a smile that made his Southern drawl sound all the more charming. "You think the Goodmans would mind if I used one o' them hand towels over yonder to dry my hands?"

"No," the concierge said, turning around to grab the towel for the workman.

Before he could turn back around, the workman snatched the

towel from his hand and placed it over the concierge's face. The young man tried to scream, but the sound came out as a muffled gag. He tried kicking his legs and flailing his arms, but the workman pushed the towel into his throat and wrestled him to the ground. The young man's face turned red, then purple, then white as his life wasted slowly away. In two minutes, he was still. And now the real work would begin.

Troy Williams took off the glasses and baseball cap he'd taken from Old Man Williams. Then he looked at his watch. He figured Renaldo would be back soon after realizing that the call Troy had made about his wife was a hoax. That meant that Troy had just a few minutes to search the condo Duane Faison had used as a safe house.

Troy knew that this was the last place Chuck had taken Duane and he knew that the police had missed the unit altogether after Duane died. They'd virtually stopped trying to trace his final hours after he confessed to the murders of the politically connected drug dealer Rafiq and his driver. After all, they'd already linked him to the murders of his brother and his best friend, they'd recovered his three-million-dollar cocaine shipment from the truck behind the mall, and they'd confiscated the five hundred thousand in cash that he was carrying when he died. As far as the police were concerned, the case was closed.

But Troy had done his research, and he knew that they'd merely scratched the surface of Duane's wealth. There was an offshore bank account containing over five hundred thousand dollars, and a villa in the hills of St. Croix. There was a life that Duane had set up for himself and Karima, and if Troy could find the account and routing numbers, he would use a portion of the money to carry out the murders he had planned. With the remainder, he'd live the life Duane had planned to live for himself.

Since the police had found only money and a gun on his body, Troy believed that Duane had accidentally left the account numbers behind. Duane could have hidden them in his Society Hill apartment or in the cars that his brother had secured for him. If, as Troy suspected, Duane was planning to leave with Karima on the day he died, the safe house was the most logical hiding place.

Troy picked up his monkey wrench and bashed a hole in the living room wall. Quickly, he reached into the space behind the Sheetrock and searched it. He did that four more times as he rampaged through the living room. The dining room was next, then the bedroom.

He stood with chest heaving, exhausted from the ten-minute search, and went back to the kitchen where the body of the young concierge grew cold.

He dropped the monkey wrench into the toolbox and bent down to retrieve it. That was when he saw a piece of paper sticking out from beneath the counter. It had been ripped from a calendar in March—a little over a month before the mayor and Duane were killed.

The piece of paper didn't contain the numbers Troy was looking for, but there was a name: Regina Brown, with a time, seven o'clock, and a phone number with a City Hall extension. It was circled along with the date, April 27. Duane had drawn a dollar sign next to the name.

Troy immediately recognized the name. She was the woman Chuck had told him about, the one Duane had met there to talk about money. As chief clerk of Philadelphia's City Council, and a good friend of Marilyn Johnson's, Ms. Brown would be easy to find.

He stuffed the paper into his pocket, picked up the toolbox, and walked calmly into the hallway, pulling the baseball cap low over his eyes and heading for the stairs. A few curious neighbors had come to their doors after hearing the racket in the empty condo.

One of them, a woman of about seventy whose television was her only company, thought she recognized the man beneath the baseball cap, glasses and work clothes as the ice-pick–wielding criminal she'd seen on the news. But things like that didn't happen there, and her eyes weren't as good as they used to be. She told herself that the man she'd seen was Renaldo, the maintenance man.

Her false sense of security allowed her to feel safe in spite of herself. It also allowed Troy to leave Cherry Hill and return to Philadelphia for his own special meeting with chief clerk Regina Brown.

6.

Karima and Kevin Lynch burst through the doors of the intensive care unit of Hahnemann Hospital and walked quickly past the police officer guarding Sharon Thomas's door.

When they walked into her room, a doctor was standing in front of Sharon's bed, checking her vitals and obstructing their view. When he moved, Karima froze at the sight of her mother with so many tubes attached to her suddenly frail-looking frame. Lynch reached out and held Karima's hand, steadying her. Then Sharon opened her eyes and looked over at the two of them. Karima quickly composed herself, not wanting her mother to see her looking so frightened.

The doctor walked over to Karima. "You can stay here with her for a few minutes," he said in the grave tone that doctors use when life hangs in the balance. "No more than that."

"Will she make it?" Karima asked.

The doctor looked back at Sharon before looking Karima in the eye. "I wish I could tell you that for sure."

He nodded a curt greeting to Lynch before walking out the door and into the hallway. Lynch watched him leave. Karima watched her mother.

Sharon smiled weakly. Karima returned the gesture, then moved quickly to her mother's bedside.

"How are you, Mom?" Karima asked, trying and failing to sound upbeat.

Sharon closed her eyes tightly and touched Karima's face as a tear made its way down Sharon's cheek. "I'm fine now," she said, opening her eyes. "As long as you're home, I'm fine."

"We're gonna find the man who did this to you, Mom. You know that, don't you?"

The beeping of the heart monitor in the corner of the room began to quicken as Sharon's heart rate increased. Karima was about to push the button for the nurse when her mother reached out and grabbed her hand with a grip that was surprisingly strong.

Karima looked back at Lynch, unsure of what to do.

"Ms. Thomas, we need to know the identity of the man who was sitting next to you today in court," Lynch said.

He reached into his breast pocket and pulled out a blurry still photo taken from the truTV video of the day's proceedings. "Do you recognize him?" Lynch asked.

Sharon looked at it and turned abruptly away. Her body tensed and her eyes filled with tears as she held back sobs too painful to release. Then she turned slowly to face Karima, and summoned all the strength she had left to finally tell the truth.

"He just showed up out of nowhere," Sharon said, her eyes staring into the past. "I guess I should have known he would someday, but I told myself that once I let it go, he would, too."

"What are you talking about, Mom?" Karima asked, her tone urgent. "Just tell us who he is."

"I never wanted you to suffer the things I did," Sharon said. "That's why I fought so hard to keep you away from Duane. I didn't want to see you get hurt the way I got hurt with Bill."

She stopped and breathed in deep, her back arching slightly as she fought to catch her breath. Karima touched the back of her hand and rubbed it gently.

"But we can't choose who we love," Sharon said. "We just do. If that love is real, there's nothing in the world that can match the feeling. We take love and hold it tight, even when we know that the cost of love's pleasure is unimaginable pain."

Sharon looked up at Lynch and then stared into her daughter's eyes. "I still remember the way Bill's eyes lit up when I told him I was pregnant," she said with a smile. "I thought he'd leave Marilyn and spend the rest of his life with me, but Marilyn had one last trick up her sleeve. A few days later, when he told me that we could never see each other again, the light in his eyes was gone."

"What does this have to do with the man sitting next to you today?" Karima asked.

"There were two of you," Sharon said. "Fraternal twins. The day you were born I was in the delivery room alone. No family, no friends, no one except a doctor and nurse. I think that's what finally made me snap. I looked at these two little babies, and in your face I saw myself—a victim of men, of family, of everyone. In your brother's face I saw all the men I'd ever hated and the only man I'd ever loved. I know now that I wasn't thinking rationally, but I couldn't bear the sight of a boy who reminded me of all I'd lost. I gave him up for adoption." The tears began to flow more quickly. "And I held on to you."

"Are you saying—"

"The man you saw beside me today was your brother," Sharon said, turning away from her.

"How do you know?" Karima asked. "Maybe there was some kind of mistake. Maybe—"

"When he sat down beside me and said, 'Hi, Mom,' I looked at him and he had your eyes. It was the only thing about the two of you that was identical when you were born.

"He asked if he could talk to me in the hallway, and I knew I owed him at least that. Then he said he never forgave me for giving him away. I don't know that I blame him."

Sharon broke down, her body shaking as the sound of her sobs filled the room. Karima hugged her and whispered sounds of forgiveness in her ear, but Sharon would not be consoled.

"I gave him away!" she screamed as the doctor ran into the room. "I gave my baby away!"

The doctor tried to pull Karima away from her mother. The heart monitor in the corner of the room beeped faster as Sharon's pulse increased. Sharon cried out in pain as she went into cardiac arrest.

Two nurses ran into the room and surrounded Sharon along with the doctor as Karima backed slowly away. "I love you, Mom," Karima whispered again and again. "I forgive you."

They lubricated the defibrillator and ripped Sharon's gown from her body as Lynch tried to pull Karima away from her mother's bed.

"Clear!" the doctor shouted as they shocked her repeatedly.

From the looks of her, it was clear that Sharon had already felt her last pain. When the beep of the heart monitor turned into a steady tone, she was dead.

Karima now knew what had always been missing in her life. The twin with whom she had shared Sharon's womb was the part of her that she'd been looking for all this time.

She thought of the loneliness her brother must have experienced without her. She asked herself if things could have been different had they known one another. But of all the questions she had about him, the one that kept coming to the surface was: Why?

Somewhere down deep, she knew. He'd done it for the same reasons that Sharon had locked herself away from the pain she had caused. In the same way that she escaped the past by hiding from it, he escaped the past by trying to eliminate it.

Karima wept with anger and grief as she watched the doctors pull the sheet over her mother's face. When she reached up to dry the tears from her eyes, the measure of sympathy she'd felt for her brother disappeared. It was replaced with the same simmering hatred that had allowed him to murder their mother.

She knew in that moment that the brother whom she'd never met would come to know her intimately now, because Karima planned to do far more to him than he'd ever dreamed of doing to their mother.

City Hall was quiet, except for the constant chatter of television sets following the day's events. Since Tatum's murder and Marilyn's rapid descent, City Hall was always quiet.

Now that the power had fallen into the hands of so-called reformers, the old guard was waiting for the other shoe to drop.

Almost none of them remembered that they'd once been reformers, too. If they had, they would have known that reform almost always ends up as nothing more than a polished version of the status quo.

City Council chief clerk Regina Brown was one of the few who had figured it out. However, Regina was a rare breed. Yes, she was the daughter of a former city councilman, and she'd gotten her City Hall job the way the relatives of politicians often did.

Regina was unique. Not in the way she looked. Her face was doughy, with no feature more prominent than the next. Her skin was the color of a brown paper bag. Her shape was like that of a large bell. But as plain as she was, the forty-five-year-old chief clerk had something that was rare in most people who'd had things handed to them.

Regina was an observer.

She'd watched her father, who, along with Marilyn's father, was one of the first blacks to hold real political power in Philadelphia. She'd seen him straddle the line between doing for the black community and doing for himself. Then she'd watched him cross that line altogether.

As a child, Regina had believed that her father, a rambunctious at-large councilman, could do no wrong. She listened to his impassioned speeches on the campaign trail, and watched as the poor blacks of North Philadelphia's ghettos cheered him wildly. She trembled on those rare occasions when she'd miss school to watch him debate on the floor of the council, fighting for this cause or that. She was awed when his speech ended and applause would echo from the wood and marble walls.

For years, she believed that the speeches were changing things for everyone. After all, they'd changed things for her family.

Her father's position had allowed them to be spoiled by extravagant gifts, even as the special interests that owned him were showering him with cash-filled envelopes. Her father's political clout bought Regina and her sisters admittance to the finest schools, and bought her mother's silence about her husband's extramarital affairs with the secretaries who worked for him.

Somewhere along the way, Regina, the little girl who'd observed the creation of black political power, grew into the woman who despised it.

In the twenty years her father had been on the council, the black neighborhoods he represented went from bad to worse. Quiet speakeasies were replaced by open-air drug markets. Street fights gave way to murders. The hopes of a generation drowned in the excess of the black political elite. And still, her father did nothing.

She often wondered why her father, with all his power, couldn't change the circumstances of the poor blacks who'd elected him to office. During his life, he'd often see that very question in her eyes. Before he died, he did the only thing he could do to answer it. He brought her into the cesspool that was City Hall, and allowed her to see the truth for herself.

In the fifteen years since her father's passing, she'd learned it all too well. While working her way up from typist to chief clerk, she'd watched every bill the council generated wind its way through the legislative process.

She saw various council presidents assign bills to committees where they knew they'd never get a hearing. When they did get hearings, Regina was the one who typed the hearing notices. She was the one who reviewed the witness lists. She even made it her business to read over the hearing transcripts.

She paid special attention to the bills that were meant to help poor neighborhoods, and she saw what happened when those bills came up for council votes.

Even when the black council members came together, they could never quite eke out the nine votes they needed to pass the legislation. Whenever they did, the mayor would veto it for budgetary considerations.

The city, after all, could never help its poorest residents. There were too many needy corporations more deserving of taxpayer money.

Oh yes, Regina knew the system all too well. On this morning, with a killer on the loose and the federal investigation of City Hall moving rapidly toward its conclusion, Regina knew it was time for her to make her move.

She'd long ago stopped being that idealistic little girl who thought that politics could change everyone's lives. Instead, she'd settled for a reality that said that politics could change hers.

As far as she knew, no one, including Marilyn, knew anything about the enterprise Regina had established nearly fifteen years ago. She'd always been good with numbers. And for years, Regina had leaned on the connections her father had established on the street in order to make her fortune. She showed drug dealers and numbers runners how to make their money legitimate. She used fake names and shell companies to establish offshore bank accounts for them. She used courier services, wire transfers, and online accounts to move the money out of the country. She used her knowledge of city government loopholes to make sure that even the girlfriends and relatives who kept the dealers' property in their names would never have to pay taxes.

In return, Regina Brown took a 10 percent fee from every transaction. Over the last fifteen years, that had amounted to over $2 million, including the interest. If she combined that money with the half-million that Duane Faison had left behind in the offshore bank account she'd established for him, she could live comfortably in the islands for the rest of her life. And that was exactly what she intended to do.

"I'm going across the street to get some coffee from Dunkin' Donuts," she said to one of the typists working in her office. "You want anything?"

"No," the woman said. "Thanks, though."

"Okay, I'll be right back." Regina picked up her pocketbook and looked back at her vast office, with its metal file cabinets and manila folders lining the walls.

She walked down the hall to the elevator and took it down to the first floor. Instead of walking toward the coffee shop, she went out the other entrance and walked to her reserved parking space across from City Hall to get into her car.

Sighing heavily, she looked in her purse for the card where she kept the combination to the safe containing the account numbers. Suddenly she felt something cold and hard press against the back of her neck.

"Scream and I'll kill you," a calm male voice said from the back seat.

Regina stiffened. She'd always known a moment like this would come, having dealt with the kinds of people she did. As the stiffness gave way to uncontrollable shaking, Regina cried.

"What do you want?" she said, cutting her eyes at two police officers walking outside City Hall.

"I want you to be smart," the voice said. "You could yell for those cops and neither of us would make it out of this car alive. Or you can do what I say and at least you'd have a chance."

Regina looked in the rearview mirror, but couldn't see him. "Who are you?" she asked, her voice shaking.

"You don't really want to know that, Ms. Brown," he said frankly. "Because then it'd be harder for me to let you live."

"So what do you want with me?" she asked.

Troy rose from the back seat with the baseball cap pulled low over his face. "I want Duane Faison's account and routing numbers," he said in a friendly tone. "And then I want you to help me with my list."

"What list?" she asked, sounding even more afraid.

"I'll tell you all about it soon enough," Troy said, smiling. "First, we need to get out of here."

Regina started her red Buick, pulled out of the space, and started down JFK Boulevard. As she did, she took one last look back at City Hall, and wondered if she'd ever see it again.

They'd taken Chuck's body over an hour ago, and the crowd outside the rooming house consisted mostly of reporters. As their news vans sat perched on nearby sidewalks with satellite dishes hoisted in the air, the police went about their business.

Ten cops from the Crime Scene Unit were sweeping Chuck's

apartment for evidence that would indicate how the killer had accessed the rooming house, and what he had left behind.

Passersby occasionally stopped to make faces for the cameras, but not many of them paid attention to the cops. Most people were so accustomed to the constant presence of crime scenes that they simply walked by without so much as a backward glance.

Skeet, who'd returned after talking with Mr. Vic, was more interested in the cops than the other observers. He sat on the steps of a nearby abandoned house with a detached expression on his face. He seemed to be looking at everything but the crime scene.

To the media, he was invisible. The cops ignored him as well. He looked like the aimless boys they saw every day in neighborhoods like this one, boys whose idle days were nothing more than preparation for lives that would be spent in prison cells. Patrolman Thurman Blackston didn't ignore him. He took notice because he was much more in tune with the streets than the others.

In the three years Blackston had been on the force, he'd learned two things: he hated being a cop, and he hated being broke. He stopped arresting the dealers in the sector he patrolled, and offered them his services in exchange for weekly payments. Duane and Glock were dead now. Heads was now his primary employer.

While the arrangement had worked out well for him thus far, Blackston wasn't a careful man. His car was too expensive, his house was too big, and his clothes were too flashy. People were starting to notice. Blackston was beginning to feel like it was only a matter of time before he was caught.

He didn't want that time to come today.

Having already relayed all the information he knew about

Chuck's stabbing to Skeet earlier, Blackston didn't plan to speak to him again—at least not out in the open, where reporters and other police officers could see. However, he had been assigned to guard the front of the building, and it was difficult for Blackston to avoid the boy.

Once Skeet realized that, he got up from the steps and sauntered across the street to get the information he needed. Unlike Blackston, he couldn't afford to wait.

"Excuse me, Officer," he said in a voice that was a bit too loud.

"Back up, son," a white officer standing guard with Blackston said. "This is a crime scene."

"I was talkin' to him," Skeet said, pointing to Blackston.

"Well, I was talkin' to you," the cop said, while stepping aggressively toward the boy.

Two television reporters took notice of the building tension. As cameramen prepared to shoot the scene, Blackston stepped between the other cop and the boy.

"It's okay," he said, too low for the reporters to hear. "I think he's got some information he might want to give us. Gimme a minute."

The white cop looked at both of them as if he wanted to say something more. Then the television reporters looked at him, and he thought better of it. Blackston grabbed Skeet by the arm and pulled him nearly ten feet away.

"This better be good," Blackston mumbled, sounding annoyed.

"Heads need to know everything y'all got right now," Skeet whispered. "He can't wait 'til later."

Blackston looked around self-consciously. The white officer

was watching him suspiciously. The television reporters were lurking nearby. Blackston smiled nervously before taking out a pen and notepad and turning back to Skeet to act as if he were interviewing him.

"I need to hear that from Heads," he said while jotting down gibberish on the notepad.

Skeet sighed impatiently and snatched his cell phone from his pocket. "You wanna talk to him? Call him. Tell him you ain't doin' what he payin' you to do. When Heads start makin' calls, though . . ." Skeet paused to look around at the cops and reporters on the scene. "You might start gettin' some questions you don't wanna answer."

Blackston looked down at the boy, knowing that if he were exposed he would go directly to jail, where he would pay the ultimate penalty long before he could serve whatever sentence he received. He had no intention of facing that fate, and Skeet knew it.

Blackston took the bluff. He didn't have any other choice.

Looking at the boy with a disdain that bordered on outright hatred, the cop pursed his lips and jotted more notes on his pad.

"They knew each other," the cop whispered after a long pause. "There was no sign of forced entry, and the two of them sat down at a table in the corner of the room at some point before the struggle began. The guys on the Crime Scene detail don't think they'll get any clean fingerprints, but there was blood spattered near the table and the bed. They're hoping some of it belongs to the killer."

"Is that all?" Skeet asked.

Blackston looked around uncomfortably. "There was one more thing."

"What?"

"The victim had a bag packed. It looked like he might have been about to skip town."

Skeet idly wondered if Chuck and the killer had been working together on a con of their own. He also wondered something else.

"Was any money in the bag?" Skeet asked.

"Just clothes, I think."

Skeet looked up at him as if he were waiting for more.

"That's all I know," Blackston said, looking around nervously.

A car pulled up and paused in front of the house before easing around the corner and parking on the sidewalk.

Skeet glanced at the black Mercury as he spoke to Blackston.

"Let me know if you find out anything else," he said, his eyes drifting as he craned his neck to see who would emerge from the car. "Heads countin' on you."

The cop put away his notepad and started to walk away. As the occupants of the black Mercury got out of the car, he also paused to see who they were. A few seconds later, when everyone there saw their faces, there was a moment of silence, and then the voices of the media erupted all at once.

Reporters surrounded the man and woman who were walking quickly toward the house. They fired questions that neither of them seemed prepared to answer.

"Captain Lynch, in what capacity is Karima Thomas here?" asked a reporter from the *Daily News*. "Is she a witness?"

Lynch and Karima pushed through the crowd without responding.

"Have you established a positive link between the courtroom

stabbing and this one?" asked a reporter from the *Philadelphia Metro*.

They approached the steps without answering.

"Karima, why are you here instead of at the hospital with your mother?" said a reporter from Channel 3. "Isn't she in critical condition?"

She stopped in her tracks. Then she wheeled on him with fire in her eyes as Lynch instinctively put an arm around her shoulder. What they'd seen at the hospital had created a bond between them. That bond allowed Lynch to see beyond the beauty that had rendered him speechless back at the prison. It made him protective. It made him possessive. It unleashed Karima's boldness.

"I just left the hospital," she said, her voice trembling with anger. "My mother died from her injuries twenty minutes ago, and I'm here to make sure somebody pays for that."

There were audible gasps from the reporters who were gathered at the scene. Some grabbed their cell phones and called their newsrooms. For two seconds, there was silence. Then the questions came again.

"So now it's murder," the *Metro* reporter said matter-of-factly. "But how can you make somebody pay? I mean, you're out on bail yourself. There's only so much you can—"

"I'll do it however I have to," she said, the threat of violence simmering just beneath her words.

As the reporter fumbled for a follow-up question, Karima turned and walked into the rooming house.

"Captain Lynch!" the reporters called out.

Lynch ignored them and followed Karima inside. Skeet melted into the crowd, his mind racing.

He knew that whomever Mr. Vic wanted to get to bring down Heads could not be as good as Karima. She was smart, bold, beautiful, and ruthless enough to do what it took to get whatever she wanted.

Skeet knew that Karima Thomas could operate on the streets, just as she'd done when the mayor was murdered. He just needed to know if she was willing to do it again.

If she was, they both could benefit. But if the body language he'd seen between her and the cop was real, Skeet would have to find someone else, and he'd have to do it quickly.

7.

"Hey, Schmidt, take a look at this," a Crime Scene lieutenant with red hair and pale skin said to a sergeant who was working nearby.

The brown-haired cop came over to Chuck's blood-spattered bed as the lieutenant pulled on rubber gloves and poked the thin mattress with his finger. There was a rustling sound, like there was paper inside.

"You hear that?" the lieutenant said.

"Yeah," the sergeant said, pulling out a knife.

He cut the stitching at the seam and carefully reached in with his gloved right hand. He removed a stack of new twenty-dollar bills from the mattress. The bank band around it said that it was a thousand dollars. The sergeant reached in again and found three more just like it.

"You think maybe our killer was looking for this?" the sergeant said as he bagged and labeled the cash.

"That's motive," the lieutenant said dismissively. "That's for Homicide to figure out."

Just then, there was a tapping at the open door. The officers turned around and saw Kevin Lynch standing on the other side of the crime scene tape. The red-eyed young woman standing beside him looked more like a model than a cop. Both she and Lynch wore expressions that made them look far more intent on solving the crime than anyone else in the room.

"This is Karima Thomas," Lynch said to the lieutenant as he and Karima entered. "She's going to be working with us on this investigation."

"I gathered that from what the reporters were saying outside," the lieutenant said, looking Karima up and down suspiciously. "Having her work on the investigation is a bit unorthodox, isn't it, Captain?"

Lynch glared at him. "Maybe if we had officers who thought out of the box instead of compartmentalizing everything, Ms. Thomas wouldn't have solved the mayor's murder before we did."

"With all due respect, Captain, she killed people in the process," the lieutenant said. "That's not the way we're doing things now, is it?"

Lynch moved quickly across the room and stood nose-to-nose with the lieutenant. "This is a homicide," he said firmly. "That means it's up to me to decide how we do things. Is that understood?"

The room went silent as the other officers turned around to see what the response would be.

The lieutenant looked at Lynch, saw the fire in his facial expression, and gave in to the higher-ranking officer. "Understood, Captain," he said, lowering his eyes.

"Good," Lynch said, looking past the lieutenant and surveying the room. "So, what do we have here? Anything new?"

There was a moment of awkward silence as the Crime Scene officers decided who would speak. "It looks fairly cut and dried," the sergeant said, speaking up. "The killer knew the victim. He let him in. The two talked here at this table."

Karima left Lynch's side and walked over to the table. She was about to touch it when one of the Crime Scene officers stopped her and handed her a pair of rubber gloves. They all watched her put them on as the sergeant went on with his scenario.

"We think the victim went for a gun that was somewhere near the bed, possibly on or under the mattress. There was a struggle. The weapon discharged twice. The killer stabbed the victim in the cerebellum, killing him instantly."

Karima walked silently through the room, looking at the bullet casings on the floor, the slugs in the wall, the scuff marks on the floor near the bed.

"Anything else?" Lynch asked.

"Yes," the sergeant said. "We found about four thousand dollars stuffed in the mattress."

"That might be confirmation that our victim was selling drugs for this guy Heads," Lynch said. "Word on the street is that the crack we found in the car crash belonged to him."

He paused for a moment and furrowed his brow. "Why would a man who'd just committed a murder come to North Philly to rob some small-time hustler for a few thousand dollars?"

"Because he didn't come for money," Karima said, speaking up for the first time as she looked out the open window he'd used to make his escape.

"How can you be so sure?" Lynch asked.

"You don't come to rob a drug dealer with an ice pick," Karima said saucily.

"Desperate people do desperate things," Lynch said. "Especially for money."

"If he needed money, he would've come here first instead of stabbing my mother in a courtroom," Karima said without a hint of emotion. "He came here for something else."

"Something like what?" Lynch asked.

Karima closed her eyes tightly as she thought it through. She was quiet for almost half a minute. Everyone else was quiet, too, waiting for what she might say.

Finally her eyes snapped open. "He must've known."

"Known what?" Lynch asked anxiously.

"Chuck was Duane's driver. He took him places no one really knew about except for him and Duane. If the killer knew that, maybe he'd want to find out where those places were."

Lynch looked confused. "Duane's dead," he said. "Why would it matter to this guy where Duane went when he was alive?"

Karima felt a chill go through her body. "Because he wants to know the best place to find someone who was close to Duane," she said, her voice firm and unafraid. "Me."

Everyone in the room knew instantly why Karima was there. She brought a perspective that none of them could, and though there were those who still didn't like it, there was no one who didn't respect it.

"I'm going to need your people to wrap this up and secure the scene," Lynch said to the lieutenant as he and Karima started toward the door. "If Karima's hunch is right, we've got a killer on our hands who's not quite through."

The two of them left the room quickly, leaving the crime scene officers to their work. As they walked down the hallway toward the steps, Karima thought of Sharon.

"When are you going to tell someone what my mother said about the killer being her son?" she asked.

"I sent a text message to a couple guys I can trust," Lynch said as they jogged down the steps. "They're getting a warrant to check Marilyn's home and office for the journal she inherited from your grandfather, and they're checking out the birth records on you and your brother."

Karima was about to respond, but as they emerged from the building, a group of reporters surged forward shouting questions they could hardly hear. Not that it mattered. Neither Karima nor Lynch had any intention of answering, and the cops guarding the building's entrance were not going to allow the media to get close to them again.

As Lynch and Karima moved toward the car, Karima felt someone staring at her. She turned and saw that it was a boy. She was about to turn away when she saw the knowing look in his eyes. It stopped her in her tracks.

The boy walked slowly toward her, and the black cop guarding the scene let him get past. Before she knew it, the boy had slipped a note into her hand and faded into the crowd of reporters.

Lynch was at the car by the time he realized that Karima wasn't beside him. She looked over at him as he waved her toward the car, then looked down at the note the boy had given her.

"Meet me at the 26th Street Speakeasy at three o'clock," it said. "I know how to find the man who killed your mother."

Karima's heart began to beat faster, and she tried desperately not to let her facial expression betray the note's importance.

Slowly, she looked up, her eyes scanning the crowd for the boy. All she saw were the cameras' bright lights and the reporters' eager faces.

Karima stuffed the note into her purse, knowing that she had no choice but to meet the boy on his terms. As she walked to the car to rejoin Captain Kevin Lynch, she knew she'd have to meet the boy by herself.

Heads had paid good money to furnish the sixtieth-floor condominium on Philadelphia's Avenue of the Arts with everything he needed. The money had bought him a view that was dazzling, both inside and out.

Holding a Cuban cigar and swilling malt liquor from a brandy snifter, he lay naked in a chaise longue, eyeing the bare-chested blonde who was next to him.

Her body was like that of a black woman—thick and curvaceous. Her eyes were green, like the condo's cushioned furniture and heated marble floors. Her lips were ample, and she used them to pleasure him in ways he could rarely resist. She'd learned much as a stripper before Heads had snatched her from the stage of one of the city's premier gentlemen's clubs, and she used every bit of it to hold on to Heads and his money.

But nothing she did could hold Heads's attention at that

moment. Even as his eyes moved from her voluptuous body to the startling view of nearby skyscrapers, his mind kept returning to the streets.

His corner had been shut down for hours because the stolen drugs had connected him to the stabbings. He'd seen the killer's picture on television and received countless leads from crackheads. One of the cops on his payroll had offered Heads the only tip that mattered. Homicide detectives were looking to speak with him. So unless he was willing to talk, he should disappear as quickly as possible.

He'd followed the advice. Now, as he looked out the floor-to-ceiling window and stared down at the office workers, power brokers, and hangers-on who gave life to the city's nerve center, he was anxious to get back to his own corner of the world. There, the action was at a standstill.

Heads was losing two thousand dollars an hour. And while the loss of the five-thousand-dollar package that Troy had taken from Chuck was no small thing, getting the corner up and running was more important.

The nubile young blonde could feel the tension in his body. It was her job to ease it. If she couldn't, Heads could just as easily go back to the strip club and find someone who could. She had no intention of letting him do that.

Lifting her head from his chest, she kissed his neck. Then she ran her tongue down to his navel, placed her hand between his legs, and caressed him.

His body began to respond, and he squeezed his eyes shut as the troubles of the day faded beneath her touch. Within moments, he was clutching her hair and guiding her mouth toward his favorite spot. Just as he was about to give in to the moment, his cell phone rang.

He reached for it with one hand and held her hair tightly with the other. The number on the screen told him that he should take the call, while his loins told him he should take the girl.

Heads did both.

"Speak," he said, half-listening as the blonde brushed his thighs with butterfly kisses.

"They got pictures o' the dude that killed Chuck," Skeet said, his tone calm as he paced the floor of his bedroom with Mr. Vic sitting nearby.

"I seen that," Heads said as the blonde began to lick him.

"They found the pack, too. Some ho out the park had the dude car. She crashed it tryin' to run from the cops. And Chuck had a bag packed, and—"

"Look," Heads said, panting as the woman's lips enveloped him. "Gimme . . . somethin' . . . I . . . can use."

Skeet could hear the girl bringing Heads to the edge of ecstasy, but as Skeet surveyed his own surroundings in the crumbling speakeasy, he knew that he was on the brink of hell.

It was high time that the two switched places.

"All right," Skeet said as Mr. Vic urged him on. "I'ma give it to you straight. Cops and news cameras posted up on Stillman Street. Smokers goin' down Thirtieth Street gettin' yellow bags from Cheese and them. If somebody don't find that dude soon, you gon' have to move your corner, and that's gon' mean a war."

Even through the fog of his arousal, Heads knew that he didn't have the manpower or strategic capacity to wage a war like the one Duane Faison had waged against Glock. As much as he wanted to wield the kind of power Duane had, taking out an entire corner was beyond his capabilities.

"Get out there and find him, then," Heads said as the girl straddled him. "I'll take care o' the rest."

"I can't do that," Skeet said simply.

The heavy breathing ceased as quickly as it had begun. "Fuck you mean you can't?" Heads said as he roughly knocked the girl to the floor.

"I gotta work through somebody else," Skeet said coolly. "Somebody who want payback as much as you do."

"Who?" Heads shouted as his patience began to run out.

"Karima Thomas."

"You mean Cream?" he whispered almost reverently.

"Yeah," Skeet said in the same hushed tone. "Cream."

Heads got up from the chaise longue and walked across the condo's living room as the blonde watched from the floor. Although the girl didn't know what "Cream" meant, she saw the way Heads's demeanor changed, and surmised it was the name of a woman.

The seconds ticked by and Skeet waited silently on the phone, knowing that this was the moment of weakness that Mr. Vic had instructed him to play upon.

Heads thought of the times he had seen Karima and Duane together. He contemplated the air she had about her—an air that Heads had never seen in the women with whom he dealt. Cream had a quiet confidence that came with her stunning physical attributes, a sense of class that grew from her upper-crust roots, and a courageousness that went beyond the gold-digging loyalties of the girls he knew. He had always wanted Karima for himself. If she could help him to reclaim his corner while he worked to make her his own, so much the better.

"She know the dude that did it?" Heads asked.

"Yeah," Skeet said, unaware of how close to the truth he was. "She been workin' with the cops, so she know where to find him, too. She ain't tryin' to wait for no warrants and arrests and shit. She want him to pay for killin' her mom, and she want him to pay now."

"She gon' bring him to me today?" he asked.

"Yeah," Skeet said. "She want the money you said you was gon' pay up front. After that, y'all can talk about whatever. You know, wit' her mom and her man dead, she might need more than a couple dollars. She might need a shoulder to cry on."

Heads's face creased in a crooked smile as he imagined what it would be like to have everything he wanted, including Cream.

"I'll call you at three-fifteen," he said as the blonde he'd cast aside looked up at him with jealousy in her eyes. "I'll tell you where to bring Cream to meet me."

After Heads disconnected the call, Skeet glanced at Mr. Vic.

The old man didn't have time to heap congratulations upon the boy. He was too busy preparing to get the tools they'd need to pull it off.

Karima was barely listening as Lynch talked about the investigation on the drive to Center City. She occasionally acknowledged a question with a grunt or a nod, but she hadn't heard anything he'd said from the time the boy had approached her with the note.

Only when Lynch pulled the car into the parking lot of police headquarters did she begin to notice her surroundings, and even then, it was only because of the memories that the place brought back.

She still remembered the day she was released from her first stint in prison. Duane had met her in that parking lot in a cherry-red Mercedes, leaning back in the cream-colored leather driver's seat with his lips fixed in a grin.

His eyes were intense, strong, and observant—as dangerous as they were gentle. That day, she knew that she could never let him go.

Duane Faison was six feet two inches of trouble, and when he smiled at her, the white of his teeth against his chocolate skin looked like sunshine to Karima's weary eyes. He was her weakness. And Karima—the woman he'd come to know as Cream— was his weakness as well.

That day, she gave in to him after six months of telling herself she wouldn't, and as the rain stretched out across the morning sky, she fell in love with him all over again.

A few days later, the man of her dreams died trying to protect her. Karima felt that she had no one to blame but herself.

"Karima," Lynch said, his voice laced with concern. "Karima!"

She turned to face him.

"We're here," he said as he watched her tears streaming down. "Are you all right?"

She wiped her face quickly. "Yes," she said with a tense grin. "Just memories, that's all. I'll be fine."

"Your mother was a good woman," Lynch said.

She nodded and pursed her lips, unwilling to tell him the real source of her tears.

Lynch sat there for a moment, looking at her. The tears made her seem more vulnerable, which made her face even lovelier.

Karima looked straight ahead, refusing to acknowledge his stare in the hope that he would stop.

He didn't.

Sensing the unbridled desire in his eyes, Karima began to grow angry. At herself. At Lynch. At life.

Suddenly, she turned to him. "Why?"

Lynch was unsure how to respond. "What do you mean, why?"

"You keep trying to say you want me without saying it," she said bluntly. "I'm wondering why."

"I—I didn't realize that's what I was doing," he said, looking out his tinted windows as police officers and civilian workers walked in and out of police headquarters. "I guess I don't know why."

"I don't know, either," Karima said, the grief and anger evident in her voice. "I'll tell you what I *do* know, though. My mother's dead, my man is dead, and all I'm getting from you is some bull-shit about how you want me to help you with the case."

"I *do* want you to help me with the case," Lynch said, more to convince himself than Karima.

"No, you don't!" she said, her tone heated. "If that's what you wanted, we'd be out finding the murderer instead of sitting here trying to figure out why you keep staring at me."

She took a deep breath and calmed herself. "Look," she said, "I really am grateful for everything you've done, but I just want to find the man who killed my mother. Why don't you do us both a favor and tell me what you really want? I'll tell you yes or no, and then we can go on with our lives."

Lynch wanted to express his desire gently, but he knew that pouring his desire inside Karima's grief was like pouring salt into a wound. She'd already lost everything she'd ever cared about. Now she was clinging to the memories.

"Karima, I know Duane meant a lot to you, but—"

"Yes, he did mean a lot to me," she said, cutting him off. "More than you'll ever know."

"I understand that, but—" He paused, fumbling for his words before looking her in the eye. "Look, maybe what I'm feeling isn't real. Maybe it's just a fantasy, but I *do* want you. I shouldn't, and I'm mad at myself for not fighting it."

"*You're* mad?" she asked with a mocking laugh. "Why? Because you're married and you want me instead of your wife?"

"That's not what I'm saying, Karima."

"The two people I loved the most are dead!" she shouted before he could finish. "And from where I sit, it looks like it's all my fault. So I think I have a lot more reason to be angry than you do."

"That's not anger," Lynch said. "It's self-pity, and you're wearing it like a badge. You're stronger than that, Karima. I've seen it."

"Don't tell me I'm not angry! You can't know how it feels to lose everything!"

"Yes I can!" he shouted. Then he caught himself and lowered his voice to a near-whisper. "I feel it every time I look at my wife and see our marriage dying."

Karima thought back to the expression his wife had worn back at the prison. It was the look of a woman who was weary and neglected, the kind of look Karima never wanted for herself.

She wondered how many years it had taken for his wife to earn such misery. More than that, she wondered what it had cost Lynch to inflict it. She looked at him almost as if she felt sorry for him. Lynch avoided her eyes, afraid to look at her because he knew in his heart that he no longer wanted to fight for his marriage.

"I see your tears and I want to make them go away," he said softly. "It's like we share this sadness about everything that's gone wrong. We both have a passion for making things right. That's what I want, Karima. I want to turn the sadness into passion, and I want to share it with you. In order to do that, I have to let go, just like you'll have to let go of what you had with Duane."

At the mention of Duane, the sympathy she'd felt just moments before disappeared. She wasn't prepared to let him go yet, and she resented the fact that Kevin Lynch kept telling her to do so. Her love for Duane had been built on corners and on drug runs, in prison cells and in coded conversations. More than that, though, it had been built in the bedroom. It was more than a bond between criminals. It was a bond between a man and a woman— one that couldn't be broken by life, by death, or by Kevin Lynch.

She didn't feel the same thing that he felt. If he was willing to cast his wife aside for her after years of marriage, Karima knew that she would never respect him. That's why she felt no guilt about what she did next.

Reaching out to touch his face, she turned his chin until he was looking in her eyes. Then she reached down past her grief and found a seductive stare that rendered him defenseless.

"I'm going to need time to grieve my loss," she said, her voice low and enticing. "If you're serious about leaving your wife, you'll need time, too. Until that time comes . . ."

She moved across the seat and gently probed his mouth with her tongue. When she was finished, she backed away slowly and stroked his face with her hand.

"My answer is no," she said softly. "When this is over, if you still want me as much as you say you do, we'll see."

Lynch didn't know what to say, nor did he know how he felt. He had never so much as touched another woman in the years he'd been married to Jocelyn, yet Karima had stirred something in him. His face was so hot that he felt like he was on fire, his passions so aroused that he felt he could explode.

Unsure of what else to do, he searched her eyes to see if she meant what she'd said. As far as he could see, she did.

Lynch was blind now. Karima knew it. She had only to say the word and he would do whatever she wanted. What she wanted now was to find her mother's killer and exact her own vengeance. She didn't have time to wait for the law.

Just then, there was a loud tap on the tinted window. Startled, Lynch sat up straight before lowering it.

"Captain, I saw your car out here and I . . ." The detective stopped short when he saw Karima.

"It's okay, Detective," Lynch said as he adjusted his jacket. "What is it?"

"They'll be executing the search warrant at Marilyn's place in a few minutes."

"Is that it?"

"Actually, no. We got a strange call from Cherry Hill a couple minutes ago. A lady in Washington Commons Condominiums said she thought she saw our suspect there. She said she waited a while before calling because she wasn't sure it was him. I told her to call Cherry Hill, but she said she knew we were looking for him here, so—"

"What's the name of the building again?" Karima asked.

"Washington Commons Condominiums."

Karima felt her blood run cold. "That's the last place Duane and I went before . . ."

Lynch started the car. "Have Cherry Hill Police meet us over there," he said to the detective as he gunned the engine and sped out of the parking lot to shoot across the nearby Ben Franklin Bridge.

Karima looked at the clock on the car's dashboard and saw that it was after two. If going to the condo would lead her to the man who'd killed her mother—the brother she'd never known—she'd play on her newfound relationship with Lynch to make sure the killer never made it to trial.

If this was yet another empty lead, she'd meet the boy at the 26th Street speakeasy.

Either way was fine with Karima. It no longer mattered how she got her revenge, as long as the revenge was real.

Marilyn and Special Agent Dan Jansen took turns bathing in the downstairs powder room, neither of them speaking as they both tried to wrap their minds around the meaning of what they'd just done.

Jansen dressed quickly, walked into the living room, and glanced out the curtain at the detectives who'd been stationed outside Marilyn's home for the past hour. He poured himself two fingers of cognac from Marilyn's wet bar, then sat down and sipped slowly, lost in his own thoughts as regret began to close in on him.

Marilyn came breezing into the room wearing a pale blue cotton sundress that was a bit more modest than the outfit she'd used to seduce him.

He watched from an easy chair as she sashayed past with the thick, seductive scent of Angel radiating from her skin. She smiled each time she wore the fragrance, because "angel" was a word that almost no one would use to describe her.

Sitting down across from him, she crossed her legs. Jansen looked up at her worriedly. "Those detectives are still outside," he said, putting the cognac down on an end table and getting up to pace the floor. "I'm going out to see what they want, but I wanted to talk to you first, just in case this thing with your sister does what I think it will."

"And what's that?" Marilyn said, looking at him as if she were amused.

"It's going to cause them to look more closely at you," he said, pacing ever more furiously. "It might make them look at me, too. We don't want that. It wouldn't be good for me, it wouldn't be good for you, and it wouldn't be good for your testimony in the corruption probe."

He stopped pacing for a moment and looked at her. She'd taken off her shoes and her legs were folded underneath her. She was staring into space wearing a Cheshire cat grin that was at once bedeviling and mocking. Jansen decided to ignore it.

"I guess what I'm saying is, what happened today was a mistake," he said, sounding more like a regretful suitor than an agent assigned to protect a witness. "Not that I didn't want it to happen—I did. But I shouldn't have. I'm an FBI agent. If this was ever to come out, there's a good chance I wouldn't be that anymore. So rather than act like this is something that I can live with, I'd rather just end it now. Do you understand what I'm saying, Marilyn?"

She looked at him with eyes that seemed to laugh and scowl at the same time. "I understand it fully," she said, her tone nonchalant. "But that doesn't mean things are going to go the way you want them to."

Jansen felt himself getting angry. "Things are going to go exactly the way I want them to, Marilyn," he said firmly. "If they don't, I'm gonna have your immunity stripped away. I'm gonna have you convicted for every crooked thing you've ever done, and I'm gonna put you in jail for a very, very long time. No parole. No deals. No nothing."

Marilyn was taken aback for a moment. Then she composed herself just enough to play her trump card.

"I thought what happened today meant something to you," she said, getting up from her chair and walking across the room to the wet bar. "Now I see that it didn't. But I don't mind, because it meant even less to me."

She poured herself a cognac and ran her finger along the rim of the glass. Then she reached below the bar and removed a small black object.

Jansen watched as she walked over to him, tossed it onto a table, then crossed the room again and sat down in her chair.

Looking down, he saw that it was a videotape. He picked it up and knew without asking what it contained. Taking another sip of cognac, the agent massaged his suddenly throbbing temples between his thumb and forefinger.

"The way I see it, you have two choices," Marilyn said, still running her finger along her glass. "You can work with me and save your career. Or you can refuse and we'll both go down together."

Jansen turned pale and his hand went limp as he allowed the tape to drop to the floor.

"We look marvelous on tape," Marilyn said sarcastically. "I made a few copies while you were in the bathroom. Stored one on the computer, too."

The agent took a deep breath and sat down. "What do you want?" he asked.

"I think it's more a question of what we both want," Marilyn said as she walked over to him and sat down in his lap. "You want me to testify in the City Hall corruption probe. I want whatever questions they have about me concerning my sister to go away. I didn't have anything to do with it, and I don't need anyone digging into my personal life to try to make it seem like I did."

Jansen got up, nearly spilling Marilyn and her drink onto the floor. "You know I can't promise that."

"You're the FBI," she said, standing and touching his face. "You can promise anything you want. And since you made me feel so good today, I might just give you anything you want in return."

"Stop it, Marilyn," he said, slapping her hand away.

She grabbed his chin and made him look at her. "I don't want to be in this situation any more than you do, but using you was the only way to get what I wanted."

He pulled her hand down from his face. "You didn't have to do it this way!" he said, the veins bulging in his neck.

"It's the only way I had left," she said, calmly sipping at her cognac. "I have too many things to hide to just allow the FBI or the Philadelphia Police Department or whoever to dig through my life."

"Is that why you didn't want Karima talking to your husband?" he asked, raising his voice.

Before she could answer, there was a knock at the door.

The two of them looked at each other before Jansen went to answer it. "Who is it?" he asked with his hand on the butt of his gun.

"Philadelphia Police," came the response from the other side of the door. "We have a warrant to search the premises."

8.

Regina Brown nervously pushed the button to activate the garage door that was built into her townhouse in the city's rapidly developing Fairmount section. Each time she pushed it, nothing happened.

She was sweating as she looked into the rearview mirror at her unwelcome guest. "It won't open," she said, her voice shaking with fear. "Maybe we should just—"

"Give it to me," he said, reaching over the seat.

She hesitated, hoping that one of her neighbors would see her car sitting in front of the garage and ask what was wrong. That wasn't going to happen. It was the middle of a summer day. The busy young professionals who lived nearby weren't at home.

"Now!" he hissed, sensing that she was stalling.

She handed over the remote control and in seconds, he spotted the problem. There was a torn piece of a Post-it note stuck to the laser that activated the device. He removed it and pushed the button. The door opened and Regina drove inside.

When the garage door closed, he got out first, squeezing into the sliver of space between the car and the wall. Seeing an opportunity to get away from him, Regina locked the car door and tried to throw the car in reverse. Troy responded quickly. He smashed his fist through the driver's-side window and grabbed the keys from the ignition, dropping his gun in the process.

Regina screamed. He covered her mouth with one hand and yanked open the car door with the other. Regina bit into his palm. He grunted, but he didn't let go. She looked up and saw a flash of light brown skin beneath the baseball cap. She saw that he was tall and muscular. She saw a hint of softness in his face. It all looked familiar to her. She knew that she'd seen him somewhere before. Just as her mind was processing the memory, he grabbed her hair and tried to drag her out of the car.

She struggled mightily, using all her weight to stay inside the car, but the more she fought, the stronger he seemed to become. Before she knew it, he had her sprawled across the driver's seat.

Just as Regina was about to give up, Troy released her hair and tried to get his other hand out of her mouth. Regina bit down even harder and swung wildly with both hands. With his free hand, Troy felt along the floor of the garage until his fingers closed around the butt of the gun. She continued to struggle. Then he jammed the gun against her temple.

"Stop," he said, panting heavily. "Or I'll kill you."

Regina was breathing hard, too. Her heart was beating wildly against her chest. She felt as if she would have a heart attack. Perhaps that way she could die without having to give him what he wanted. She knew that it wouldn't play out that way. She wanted to live too much, so she reluctantly stopped biting his hand and allowed her body to go limp against the seat.

A second later, he raised his fist and brought it crashing down against the side of her head. She saw a flash of bright light as the pain shot through her body. Closing her eyes against it, she told herself that this was all a dream, though she knew that she was telling herself a lie.

Troy bent down until his lips were almost against her ear. "The Post-it you put on the garage door opener was one," he said, in a tone that was soft yet menacing. "That shit you just pulled was two. Another mistake would make three." He ran his fingers through her hair, then grabbed a fistful and yanked her head back. "You only get three strikes, Regina. After that, you're out."

He let her go and waved the gun toward the door that led into her house from the garage. She walked past him and through the door. He followed her inside.

"What if I don't have the account numbers you're looking for?" she said as she walked into the kitchen with Troy close behind.

"You die."

"I'm gonna die anyway, right? What difference does it make if I give you the account numbers?"

Troy smiled. He liked her resourcefulness. "Sit down," he said.

She took a seat at her kitchen table. She knew that she had no other choice. She also knew that if she was going to die, she was going to know who her killer was—even if she had to take his face to the grave.

Regina tried to turn around to get a good look at him, but he placed a hand on her shoulder before she could do so.

"I wouldn't do that if I were you," he said, grabbing a chair from the table, placing it behind her, and sitting down.

Regina could hear him breathing behind her, and she could see his shadow against the far wall. He looked ominous. Then she heard a faint tapping sound as droplets from Troy's bloody hand fell against the linoleum floor.

"You should wrap that," Regina said. "It might get infected."

"I need the account numbers," he said, ignoring her medical advice.

"So that's all you want is money?" she asked. "Because if that's all you want—"

"Just write down the account numbers and the routing numbers."

"It's . . . it's in the car," Regina said nervously. "In my purse."

He jumped up and was about to snatch her out of her seat when the phone rang. They both froze. The call went to the answering machine after the first ring, so they both heard the message.

"Regina, this is Pam. I called your job, but they said you went for coffee. I tried your cell, too, but it just rang. Anyway, they just said it on the news. Sharon died, girl. Ain't that somethin'? Call me when you get a chance. Bye."

The caller hung up and Regina remembered where she had seen the face of the man sitting behind her. He was the man in the blurry court video who had been sitting next to Sharon in the courtroom. He was the one who had stabbed her. Now he was wanted for murder.

She stood up on wobbly legs, turned to face him, and spoke before she could think. "You killed Sharon," she said, her brow furrowed in disbelief as she stared into Troy's eyes.

In a single motion, Troy leveled his gun at her face and grabbed her neck with his free hand. "Get the numbers now," he said, pushing her toward the garage.

Realization made her blood run cold as she stumbled backward. "You killed that man in North Philly, too, didn't you?"

"I'll kill *you* if you don't get me the numbers," he said angrily.

She tripped over a chair as she moved backward. He snatched off the baseball cap, chambered a round in the gun, and looked at her with the eyes of a maniac. She searched those eyes for a trace of humanity and found none. She knew then that she was about to die. That knowledge gave her a strange sense of peace, and a boldness she didn't know she had.

"If you're going to kill me," she said calmly, "at least tell me why."

"Because you're here!" he shouted as he opened the garage door and pushed her inside. "Because you're in my way!" he said, pushing her again. "Because people like you make it possible for people like Sharon and Marilyn and Karima to exist." He pushed her again and she fell backward against the hood of the car.

"Is that the list you were talking about?" she asked, her voice trembling as she put both hands behind her and felt her way to the driver's side of the car. "The list of people you're going to kill?"

He pointed the gun toward her face. "My list is a little longer than that."

"Then let me help you with it," she said, her tone desperate. "You said you'd let me help."

"I have to do this alone," he said ominously.

"Why?"

"I've spent my life waiting for people to help me: first my parents, then my foster parents, and now you. I don't trust people anymore. They've hurt me too many times."

Regina listened, growing more fearful with each word he spoke.

"All those people who were supposed to help me when I needed it . . . they'd better pray that God helps them now."

His eyes turned on her the same way they'd turned on his other victims in their final moments. They were filled with a mixture of rage and hatred that almost burned holes through her. Regina had never seen such a look before. It frightened her.

"Get the numbers," he said as he raised the gun to her forehead.

She reached around to open the door, but she moved too slowly. Troy grabbed her by her throat and nearly lifted her from her feet with one powerful hand. She clawed at his wrist and he let her go, snatching the door open before she could hit the ground. Jamming the barrel of the gun against the back of her head, he lifted her by her clothes and forced her into the car.

"Get the numbers now!" he said in a tone at once enraged and controlled.

Sobbing quietly, she reached into her purse and pulled out the sheet of paper that she'd thought would be her ticket to freedom. She looked at the numbers and saw every drug dealer whose money she'd ever laundered. She saw each dollar she'd ever skimmed. She saw her father ignoring the plight of the people who'd placed him in office. She saw herself.

Troy snatched the paper from her hand and examined it carefully. With those numbers, he could pay the one man who could strike the most difficult victim from his list. Though Troy regretted that he couldn't kill every one of them personally, he was glad that he had made provisions to eliminate them by other means. Soon he would make the call that would set things in motion. For now, he had other business to attend to.

Placing the paper in his pocket, he turned a terrified Regina over onto her back. He extended his arm until the gun was between her eyes. She looked down the barrel and saw blackness, then the white flash of the discharge, then the redness and the emptiness of death.

Special Agent Dan Jansen was on the phone with headquarters, trying feverishly to stop the search of Marilyn's home that had been going on for the last half hour. He'd made very little headway, because not even the federal government could instantly stop a court-ordered search—especially if there was no clear reason to do so.

"Look, I know it isn't customary for the FBI to halt the execution of a search warrant," Jansen said in an exasperated tone as he listened once again to an Assistant U.S. Attorney explain the intricacies of jurisdiction.

"Yes, I get it," he said, interrupting once again. "Can't we just get a judge to sign a cease and desist?"

The attorney explained that it would take hours to make something like that happen, even if they moved as quickly as possible.

Jansen slammed the phone into the cradle and looked around in frustration at the detectives who were busily searching the room.

He'd already told them that Marilyn was a witness in a federal investigation, and as such was under federal protection. However, the sergeant in charge of the search wasn't about to be put off. After sitting outside the house for several hours while Marilyn and Jansen were inside with the curtains drawn, he was not only suspicious of Marilyn, he didn't trust the FBI agent, either.

"Can you come over here for a minute, please, Agent Jansen?" the sergeant said as he bent over a damp spot on the carpet.

Jansen walked over to the sergeant and bent down warily, his eyes filled with the fear that he was trying so hard to hide. The sergeant smiled at him, but there was no humor in the gesture. In fact, there was no humor in the sergeant at all.

His brown face was clean-shaven and his coarse, tightly curled hair was cut in an inch-high Afro. Jansen estimated his age at fifty. From the look on his face, he'd spent about thirty of those years in the department.

"I'm not in the FBI, son," the sergeant said as he looked down at the spot on the carpet. "So I don't claim to know everything about investigation, or searches, or even crime." He looked up at Jansen. "But I know people. You wouldn't be working so hard to get us outta here if you didn't have something to hide."

Jansen's eyes cut over to Marilyn before he could stop himself. She was watching the two of them intently.

"I—I'm just trying to make sure this witness is available to testify in the federal trial on City Hall corruption," Jansen said, stumbling over his words. "We don't need her caught up in this."

"It's not your job to make sure she testifies," the sergeant said while slipping on a rubber glove. "It's your job to protect her."

"Look, I know my job," Jansen said defensively. "And I do it well."

The sergeant reached down and touched the wet spot with the rubber glove. Then he held the glove a few inches from his nose and sniffed. "Which job? Being an FBI agent, or fucking Marilyn Johnson on the living room floor?"

"I don't know what you're talking about," Jansen said, sounding more and more like a frightened little boy.

"Oh, I think you do," the sergeant said as he stood up and removed the glove. He looked over at Marilyn, who was still watching them nervously. "I think she does, too."

Seconds later, one of the detectives who'd been searching beneath the bar found Marilyn's camcorder and pushed PLAY. What he saw removed all doubt as to who was telling the truth. "Hey, Sarge," he said while glancing at Jansen, "look at this."

The sergeant walked over to the bar to look at the tape. Jansen didn't. He already knew what it contained. And as he listened to the muffled sounds of him and Marilyn having sex, he was repulsed rather than excited, because he knew that those sounds could mean the end of his career.

The front door opened and Special Agent John Kowalski nearly ran into the house. "Jansen, I think we've finally—" He stopped short when he saw Jansen's somber face. Having worked with him for years, Kowalski knew that somber was the last thing Jansen would be. "What's wrong?" he asked.

Jansen looked down at the stained carpet and said nothing. Marilyn sat on the chair and looked away from them both. Everyone in the room stopped talking, until the only sounds left were those on the tape.

Kowalski heard the muffled moans and shouts and went over to the bar to see what the detectives were looking at. When he saw it, he looked at Jansen and saw the shame on his face. He looked at Marilyn and saw something approaching guilt. Knowing that they'd all seen enough, he reached down and hit the OFF button.

Just then, a detective came running down the stairs.

"We found it," the detective said as he held a small, black, leather-bound book in his gloved hands.

"Yeah," the sergeant said as he put on a fresh pair of gloves and took the book. "We found a lot of things."

He walked over to Marilyn, who sat on the couch, tight-lipped and humiliated by the tape of her and Jansen.

"What can you tell us about this book, Mrs. Johnson?" the sergeant said gently.

She glanced at it, then looked away. "It belonged to my father. Now it belongs to me."

The sergeant flipped through the pages. It read like a *Who's Who* of Philadelphia. There were politicians and business leaders, law enforcement officials and civic leaders. Each of them had something troubling listed next to their name. Not even Sharon and Marilyn were exempt. Next to Marilyn's name were the identities of the lovers she'd taken while her father was alive. Next to Sharon's were the names of two people: Karima and Kareem.

"Who's Kareem?" the sergeant asked Marilyn.

She furrowed her brow and looked at the book. "I don't know," she said, sounding bewildered. "I never noticed that name before."

Special Agent John Kowalski stepped out from behind the bar. "That's what I came here to tell Jansen," he said, looking at his friend with pity in his eyes. "Now I guess I'll tell everyone." He cut his eyes at Marilyn. "Since we all seem to be so . . . *close*."

He pulled a picture from the file folder he was carrying. "Thanks to a lot of help from the Philadelphia Police and the Department of Human Services, we've been able to identify the man who was sitting next to Sharon Thomas in the courtroom today," he said, displaying the picture so everyone could see it. "His name is Troy Williams. Or at least that's the name he was given when he was about seven. Before that, his name was Kareem Thomas. He was born to Sharon Thomas twenty-three years ago, and he's Karima Thomas's twin."

Marilyn's jaw dropped in disbelief as Jansen pulled papers from the file and recounted Troy Williams's history.

"Sharon gave him up for adoption and kept Karima," he said while looking at the papers. "Troy went into foster care with the Williams family. That 'Chuck' guy they found this morning? He stayed at the Williams home around the same time as Troy. They knew each other.

"When Troy was about ten, somebody told the Department of Human Services that the boys were being abused. After that, Chuck bounced from foster care to jail to the streets. Troy was just the opposite. He tested through the roof on his standardized tests and got scholarships to Fulbright Boarding School and Virginia Tech. He graduated at the top of his class with a double major in criminal justice and psychology."

"So what happened to him after college?" the sergeant asked.

"He was recruited by the FBI. We waived the age and experience requirements because he was a genius. He worked for us for three years as a profiler—tracing criminal tendencies and helping us to catch the bad guys before they killed again. He was one of our top guys. He'd worked a number of high-profile cases for us, up to and including the City Hall corruption case and the murder of Mayor Tatum. He quit two months ago—right after the arrests in the Tatum murder."

Jansen felt a growing sense of dread as he listened to Kowalski. He'd never worked closely with Troy Williams, whose office was in Quantico, Virginia. But Jansen knew agents who had worked with him, and all of them agreed that Williams was the smartest man they'd ever met.

Troy's analysis of the City Hall corruption case had included a memo claiming that Marilyn's family's penchant for dysfunction made them more likely to participate in violence. Based on that memo, the FBI had allowed Troy to spend a month examining and reexamining each family member's background. Because of that research, Troy would surely have all he needed to eliminate them, if that was his goal.

Based on another memo that Jansen had seen just a week after Troy resigned, he would have the help he needed, too.

"We've gotta get to Bill Johnson," he blurted out before he could stop himself.

"What do you mean?" Kowalski said. "Johnson's safe. He's spent the last two months in Administrative Custody at the Philadelphia Federal Detention Center. As a witness in the corruption case, I'm sure he's being given special protection."

"I understand all that," Jansen said as his face turned pale. "But Troy wasn't the only one to leave the FBI abruptly. His assistant left, too. He's a guard at the Philadelphia Federal Detention Center now. Name's Reed. Josh Reed."

Kowalski's face creased with worry. Then he grabbed Marilyn and started toward the door.

"I'm taking Mrs. Johnson with me, Dan," he said sadly. The two men traded a troubled look. Neither of them said anything. The tape had said it all.

"Sergeant," Kowalski said, removing a folded sheet of paper from his inside pocket and handing it over. "Here's a one-sheet on Troy Williams. Please share it with Captain Lynch and whoever else needs to know."

He hustled Marilyn toward the door. "I'm going to the Federal Detention Center," he said. "I just hope we're not too late."

Lynch and Karima arrived at the Washington Crossing Condominiums and walked quickly through the sliding glass doors and across the empty lobby.

"There's no one at the desk," Lynch said. "Buildings like this usually have a concierge."

Karima looked at the black plastic sign on the desk. "This says he'll be back in a minute."

"We don't have a minute," Lynch said as he left the desk and ran to the elevator, with Karima following close behind.

As the elevator went up, Lynch looked at Karima and thought of the way she'd kissed him in the car. Karima's mind was somewhere else altogether. It was stuck on the last time she'd been at Washington Commons.

She'd often wondered what would have happened if she and Duane had run away and left it all behind. She'd asked herself, time and time again, if her desire to clear her name had overshadowed her love for him. She'd spent many sleepless nights replaying those final hours. Each time, she came to the same conclusion. Duane had loved her more than any man could ever love her again. Neither her mind nor her body would allow her to forget that.

Still, Karima knew that nothing could bring him back. The only thing she could do was what Duane would have done. She could win. That was what she intended to do. Winning was the reason she'd decided to string Kevin Lynch along. If he could get her close to the man who'd murdered her mother, Karima would have no problem doing the rest.

As they walked down the hall and arrived at the door of the condominium, Karima's heart raced as quickly as her mind. Thoughts of love and remembrance were mixed with those of hate and vengeance.

Lynch had no such thoughts. He was simply caught in the moment. The only thing that mattered was what was behind that door. He looked at Karima and drew his gun. Then he reached down and tried the door. It was open.

Lynch entered first, and he knew right away from the holes in the walls that whatever had happened there was already over. Still, he kept his gun drawn. They tiptoed through each room until, finally, they reached the kitchen.

Lynch saw the body on the floor and tried to shield Karima's eyes. She had already seen him, though, and there was nothing Lynch could do to hide it from her. After all, Karima already had an intimate relationship with death.

Lynch holstered his gun and bent down to examine the dead man. There was a towel in his mouth, and his eyes still bore the terror that he'd experienced in his last moments. The name tag on his blue jacket said "JIM MCDONALD."

"I guess this must be the concierge," Lynch said, lifting the victim's head and searching for signs of blood. "He asphyxiated this one instead of stabbing him with an icepick."

"Then how do we know he did it?" Karima asked.

"There were two surveillance cameras outside the building

and another one in the lobby. I'm sure we'll spot him when we review the tapes."

Lynch's BlackBerry rang as he holstered his weapon. He answered the call and the longer he listened, the more troubled his facial expression became. When the caller was finished, he mumbled, "Thanks," before disconnecting the call and turning to Karima with a look of extreme concern.

"What is it?" she asked anxiously. "What's wrong?"

"The FBI did a background check on Troy Williams. What your mother told us is true. Troy Williams is your brother. He was born Kareem Thomas."

"That's it?" Karima said. "You act like you're surprised."

"Well, there is one other thing," Lynch said, his voice filled with worry. "Troy worked for the FBI as a profiler until two months ago. He worked on the Tatum murder and did background checks on you, your family, even Duane. That means he's got everything he needs on all of you. So if he wants to track you down . . ."

Lynch allowed the words to hang in the air. Then he looked around the room with a bewildered expression on his face.

"The question is, if he already knows everything about you, what was he trying to find here?"

Karima looked around the condo and recalled the last moments she'd spent there with Duane. She remembered the preparations he'd made for their escape: the boat he had waiting at the docks; the change of clothes he had in the closet; the $500,000 in the offshore account.

She hadn't thought of that money in the two months since Duane had died. Nor had she thought of the slip of paper that

Duane had asked her to hold for safekeeping after a birthday dinner several months before.

"It's a copy of something," he'd told her when she asked what the numbers on the paper meant. "Just don't lose it. It's only one other person with those numbers besides us."

As Karima's thoughts came crashing back into the moment, she looked down at the clutch she was carrying. It was the same one she'd carried that night. She knew now, just as surely as she knew her name, that the slip of paper she'd placed in its inside compartment contained the account and routing numbers. Troy must have believed that the other copy was somewhere in the condo. That was why he'd bashed in the walls.

"Karima," Lynch said, interrupting her thoughts. "Do you know what he was looking for?"

"No," she lied. "I don't."

Before he could press her further, the mingled sounds of voices and footsteps filled the hall as Cherry Hill police officers burst into the room. Within minutes, they were speaking to Lynch about jurisdiction and extradition. The terminology alone sounded like it would slow things down, and Karima wasn't about to move slowly.

The crime scene filled up with photographers and fingerprint technicians, Crime Scene officers and detectives. Lynch was swept up in the furious flurry of activity. This was his world, and as Karima watched him in it, she knew that it could never be hers.

As if to underscore that point, the police pushed Karima farther and farther away from the body until, finally, she was standing by the door.

She looked at that door and remembered the way Duane had

pressed her against it until her resistance was washed away by the wetness that was pouring down from inside. She remembered kisses that made it impossible for her to do anything but moan. She remembered the desire as they both gave in to the moment.

Now she faced a different moment. She had to choose between two worlds. In Kevin Lynch's world, the straitlaced man who wanted her did everything right, and still only solved half the city's murders. In Karima's world, the hoodlums who wanted her did everything wrong. No one ever settled for half.

Karima slipped out the door, and with shaking fingers she fished through her purse for the slip of paper that Duane had given her all those months before. When she found it, tears stained her cheeks, but not because it gave her access to half a million dollars. She cried because that wrinkled sheet of paper was the only thing she had left that he had touched.

She placed the paper carefully back in her purse and pulled out her Trio. Then she dialed the operator and got the number of a cab company. Her mother's murderer was out there somewhere, and maybe what the boy had told her was the truth.

She would make it to the speakeasy by three o'clock. When she did, she would leave Kevin Lynch and his laws far behind. Then, with the money Duane had left for her, she'd give herself completely to the streets.

9.

The guard station at the Administrative Unit of the Philadelphia Federal Detention Center was quiet, but in spite of what was shaping up to be an easy afternoon, one of the guards found it difficult to keep still.

He repeatedly sucked in his ample gut to cross and uncross his legs. He ran his thick fingers through his brown curly hair. He fiddled with his government-issued tie and blazer as he looked at the clock.

His partner initially attributed his nervous energy to the shift change that would take place in half an hour. As sweat began to trickle down the fat guard's chin, he idly wondered if it might be something more.

Trouble at the FDC was rare. With its pristine halls and guards in ties and jackets, the facility looked more like a school than a prison. Everyone inside acted accordingly. There weren't the same dog-eat-dog rules that held sway in state facilities. Instead, there was a sort of hopelessness to it all. Part of it was born of federal sentencing guidelines that gave no chance of parole or early release. The rest of it came from the strictly enforced rules that maintained the facility's sense of order.

Hand stamps and ultraviolet rays were used to detect drug residue on visitors. Carefully constructed and supervised prisoner vocational programs were closely monitored by administrators. State-of-the-art cameras and electronic swipe cards made it almost impossible for guards to move about without being observed. And if, for some reason, one of them managed to find a way to engage in illicit or illegal activity, they would not only lose their jobs, they would be imprisoned in a facility much like the one in which they worked.

In spite of the technologically advanced safeguards that had been put in place, the FDC was run by people. And people are far from infallible.

Federal guards, like those in state and municipal prisons, could be bought. And the man who sat nervously by the phone, waiting for the call that would change his life, was one of those whose loyalties were up for sale.

He'd transferred from civilian work at the FBI only two months before, but he'd learned the ropes quickly. Despite his sloppy appearance, he was smart, he knew the timing of prisoner transfers, he knew the blind spots in the camera system, and he knew the prisoners who'd managed to carve out a living through extracurricular activities. In about five minutes, he'd put it all together. Soon after, he'd walk away from it all.

The guard pushed his pudgy fingers through his curly brown hair and crossed his legs once again, then began to chew on his fingernails.

"You all right, Reed?" his partner asked.

"It's just been a long day," he said, smiling weakly. "I can't wait to do this last transfer and go home."

Seconds later the phone rang. Officer Reed had to force himself to allow his partner to hand him the phone.

"Officer Reed," he said as he took the phone and listened to the caller's cryptic words.

The call, like every call in the facility, was monitored. He smiled, if only for a moment, before disconnecting. Then the smile gave way to streams of sweat. Now he would have to earn the money that would soon be wired into his bank account. In the process, he would have to risk everything.

He looked at his watch, then looked at his partner as he watched the prisoner being escorted down the hall and toward the Administrative Unit.

Having been returned to the prison by U.S. marshals after the meeting with Lynch and Karima at the Philadelphia Industrial Correctional Center, Bill Johnson was just about to be placed back in isolation. As the guards watched him bring dignity to shackles, they could see that he had once been a man of great importance. In many ways, he still was.

"It never ceases to amaze me how these corporate types continue to get in trouble," Reed's partner said as the guards escorting Bill Johnson pushed the button that opened the reinforced steel door to the unit.

"People are greedy," Reed said, slipping on a pair of leather and suede gloves. "They'll do almost anything for money."

The guards handed the prisoner over to the two of them, and they began the long walk down to his cell, with Reed holding one arm and his partner holding the other.

Bill Johnson ignored the guards, the shackles, and the reinforced steel doors, as he'd done every day for the past two months. Instead, he thought of the news he'd heard on his way back to the prison. Sharon was dead.

He wanted to grieve, but couldn't. He'd long ago turned off his feelings toward Sharon. The love he felt for her was too painful to carry in his heart. Instead, he carried it in a place that nobody could reach—not even himself.

Bill turned his attention to the walls of the prison's sterile hallway. After spending a lifetime without the woman he loved and the life they'd created, those walls were nothing to him. They were simply another layer of the prison he'd been in for the last twenty-three years.

Rather than trying to enter the emotional prison where he'd locked his love for Sharon, he allowed his mind to wander to a place where he was free. He thought of the conversation he'd had with his daughter, Karima. As he lurched toward his cell in shackles, he replayed the sound of Karima's voice saying the one word he'd always longed to hear—Dad.

When they were nearly at the cell, Reed stopped suddenly. "Wait a minute," he said, grabbing one eye as they entered a blind spot in the camera system. "I think I dropped a contact."

"You can get it after we secure the prisoner," his partner said, growing nervous.

"It'll only take a second," Reed said as he bent down and felt along the floor before reaching into his sock and grabbing a piece of sandpaper wrapped in plastic. "Got it."

He sprang to his feet and pretended to put the contact lens back into his eye.

"You all right now, Reed?" his partner asked.

"Perfect," he said with a grin as he unwrapped the sandpaper with one gloved hand.

The three of them walked toward the cell. When they removed Bill Johnson's shackles, Reed scraped the sandpaper along the prisoner's wrist.

"Ow!" Bill exclaimed while glaring at Reed and rubbing his wrist.

"Sorry about that Mr. Johnson," Reed said as he closed the door to the cell.

Once the two guards walked away, Reed placed the sandpaper in his pocket, careful not to touch it with his bare hands. He didn't want to expose himself to the poison on the sandpaper.

Bill Johnson had no such luxury. As he sat down on his bunk, he absently rubbed his sore wrist and thought of his conversation with his daughter. He'd watched her as she spoke, and noted that her mouth was shaped like Sharon's. She had full lips that were shaped so perfectly they could have been cut from clay.

More than what her mouth looked like, Bill remembered what she'd said when he noted that he would never have the chance to be her father.

"Never say never," was the phrase that emerged from her lips. "There's always another chance."

For the rest of his life, Bill would hold to the hope of that chance. He only wished he could have had the same chance with Sharon.

His thoughts shifted to the woman he loved, and what it had felt like to hold her all those years ago. He remembered her scent, which was faint and flowery, like a broken rose petal. Her persona was like that, too—except when they made love. In the throes of passion, she was confident and strong. She knew what she wanted, and she took it. Bill had never had another woman like her—not even his wife.

He rubbed his sore wrist as he thought of how Sharon's lips had felt on his. The memory caused his heartbeat to quicken, and he closed his eyes to lose himself in the past. He could hear the sound of Sharon's voice in his ear, telling him to touch her, and begging him not to stop.

His wrist began to throb as his heart beat even faster, pumping the blood through his veins along with the poison. He opened his eyes, and his vision was blurry. He opened his mouth to call for help, and his tongue was too thick to speak.

Bill fell to the floor with the sound of his heartbeat reverberating in his ears. The poison had now worked its way throughout his body.

Stabbing pain shot through his sides as his kidneys began to shut down. Unbearable weight bore down on his chest as his lungs refused more air. Wetness spread across the floor as his bowels and bladder gave way.

His mind ignored it all, and instead recalled the sensation of Sharon's arms around him, comforting him and loving him through the pain of their years apart.

Bill smiled, even as his heart refused to beat, and in his mind, he ran toward his own idea of heaven. Somewhere in the distance, he could see the woman he had always loved, beckoning him to join her in the place where their child had sent them.

In death, there was no Marilyn to keep them from one another.

He ran to Sharon's arms as he breathed his last, and there he finally allowed himself to rest.

As the officers from Cherry Hill secured the crime scene, Kevin Lynch went through the condo's rooms again, telling himself that he might have missed her the first three times. In his heart, he knew that she was gone.

Karima wasn't the kind of woman who would wait on a man. And despite what Lynch had told her in the car, he knew she wouldn't be waiting on him.

As he left the crime scene and went down in the elevator, his mind replayed all the things he'd said to her. He wondered if he should have said more. Then he wondered if he should have said less.

For the first time in years, Kevin Lynch—the man who'd faced down killers and brought them to justice—was unsure of himself. When the elevator doors opened and he looked down at his wedding ring, he knew why. Somewhere down deep, he still loved Jocelyn.

In his loins, though, he wanted Karima so badly that it hurt. He ran past the New Jersey state troopers guarding the scene in hopes of catching a glimpse of her. When he looked up and down the street, his hopes faded. She was gone.

His mind had been so preoccupied with finding her that he didn't see Philadelphia police commissioner Silas Bey leaning against his car. When Lynch spotted the commissioner, the captain smiled awkwardly, knowing that Bey must have seen how foolish he had looked just a few seconds before.

Bey, dressed casually in a jogging suit and sneakers, simply looked at Lynch to convey his displeasure. Though Lynch hated to admit it, Bey's stare was imposing.

The commissioner's tall frame was wrapped in black skin topped by gray hair, and his thoughtful eyes and soft-spoken manner portrayed a confidence that had come from years of experience.

"Where's your partner?" the commissioner asked in a tone that bordered on sarcasm.

"I didn't know I had one."

"Neither did I. That's why I'm here."

"Look, if this is about that lieutenant in the Crime Scene Unit, he's never liked me and—"

"I've never liked you, either," the commissioner said. "That never stopped me from working with you—even when you questioned my decision not to reveal what I knew about the federal investigation."

"Marilyn Johnson *made* you work with me," Lynch said as he recalled the one decision Marilyn had made as mayor. "You wanted to fire me."

"No, I didn't want to fire you then, but with everything you're doing now, I just might have grounds to put you on leave with intent to dismiss."

"Commissioner, I—"

"Bringing a civilian to a crime scene. Giving a civilian access to sensitive investigative information. And not just any civilian—a woman who's out on bail after being charged with weapons violations and attempted murder."

"Commissioner, I—"

"Disregarding departmental policy. Working outside your jurisdiction. Do I have to go on?"

"Commissioner, I know we've had our disagreements over the years, and I know I haven't always been the most disciplined officer on the force. But I've always gotten results, and I can get them again."

"At what cost?" the commissioner asked skeptically.

"It doesn't matter!" Lynch said in frustration.

"Yes it does!" the commissioner shouted, then reined in his emotions before he lost control. "Look, son, I've been on the force almost as long as you've been alive. In thirty-seven years, I've seen more than anyone should. I've seen hotshot young cops who put everything on the line for the job, and lost everything in the process. I've seen people bend the rules and end up getting broken. I've seen pretty girls turn officers' heads and make them lose the things that matter most."

The commissioner's eyes took on a faraway look. "I've given everything I had to this job, and it's cost me two marriages. Two of my children won't even speak to me. And for what? When they bury me, I'll have four stars on my shoulders. I'll get a twenty-one-gun salute and full departmental honors, but the only people who'll be crying will be other cops. That's no way to go out, son, and I don't want to see that happen to you."

"What do you care if it happens to me? Two months ago, you were ready to fire me. You hated me."

"No," the commissioner said in a placating tone. "I never hated you, Lynch. I didn't like you—probably because you reminded me so much of myself when I was your age. I guess you could say I didn't like *me*."

Lynch was taken aback by the commissioner's frank admission. It took him a moment to gather his thoughts. When he did, he could think of only one question to ask.

"What was it about me that reminded you so much of yourself?"

"The thing that reminded me then was your hunger. You wanted to be on top so bad you could taste it. Now, though . . ."

"Now what?"

"Let's just say people see things," the commissioner said. "And it's not just about Lieutenant What's-His-Name dropping a dime about what happened at the crime scene."

"Then what else could it be about?" Lynch asked with an edge to his voice. "Because anything beyond that is personal, and it has nothing whatsoever to do with my job."

"That's where you're wrong, Lynch," the commissioner said in a fatherly tone. "When you're running around chasing that girl with your nose wide open, it has everything to do with your job. When your wife has to chase you down at the prison just to get you to spend a couple minutes with your kid, it has everything to do with your job. When you leave a crime scene and the first person you look for is some girl instead of the murderer, it has everything to do with your job."

Lynch was quiet. There was no flip response to the naked truth.

"People see how you're acting and they talk, Lynch. Before you know it, four or five guys are lined up at your door, waiting for you to leave for this job you love more than your wife, because they're more than happy to take your place at home."

Lynch stood there, unsure of his ability to shake what he felt for Karima. He wasn't even sure that he wanted to.

"So what about my job?" Lynch asked quietly.

"Haven't you heard anything I've said to you?" the commissioner asked incredulously.

"Yes, but I—"

"Your job is safe. Go see about your family."

"What about the murderer?" Lynch asked.

"You've got the entire Homicide division, the FBI, and the Cherry Hill Police Department working on it," the commissioner said, placing his hand on Lynch's shoulder. "Check on your family. Then come back ready to work."

Troy sat at a red light in Regina Brown's car, his green work clothes stained with the blood that he'd spilled while taking the chief clerk's life.

He'd used her computer to transfer the funds to Josh Reed's account. Then he'd wiped the blood from the outside of her red Buick, pulled out of the garage, and closed the door to hide the body that was sprawled in the middle of the floor.

The time he'd taken to complete those simple steps had thrown his plan off schedule. He was now fifteen minutes behind.

Even so, Troy was pleased with the way things had gone thus far. He'd already struck Sharon, Chuck, and Mr. and Mrs. Williams from his list. Now he needed to make sure that Bill Johnson was dead, and he needed to make sure that Josh disappeared.

As the light turned green, Troy snatched Regina's cell phone from the passenger seat and dialed Josh Reed's number.

The call connected after the first ring.

"Done?" Troy asked in his typically cryptic style.

"They found him a couple minutes ago," Troy's former assistant said, his tone at once nervous and excited. "They want me to come back and file a report."

Josh Reed had no intention of going back. Having finished his shift, he was now on his way to New York's JFK Airport. In two hours, he'd be on a plane to Eastern Europe under an assumed identity. Or at least that was his plan.

In truth, Josh wasn't the greatest of planners. He wasn't the greatest of anything. Like Troy, he'd spent years standing angrily on the fringe of society—a quiet fat man who stayed in his place while learning about killers as an assistant to the FBI's top profiler.

The more cases he and Troy worked on together, the more Troy came to understand that his assistant's fascination with killers was as strong as his personal insecurities. It took less than a year for Troy to play on those insecurities and recruit Josh for his plot. The promise of $100,000 and the lure of the perfect murder were enough to convince Josh to follow Troy's lead and leave the FBI.

Now that he had carried out Troy's directions to the letter, it was up to Josh to disappear, and it was time for Troy to move on to his next target.

"Made the transfer fifteen minutes ago," Troy said. "The papers will get you out. After that, it's up to you."

"Thanks," Josh said, the gratitude evident in his voice.

When Josh hung up, Troy smiled. It would take more than luck for Josh Reed to make it out of the country. It would take a miracle, and Troy knew it.

The fake passport, driver's license, and Social Security card that Troy had provided him would be caught by customs agents, who would detain him. They would call in the FBI. While the feds touted Josh's capture as a major break in the case, the media frenzy would shift gears, Josh would feed them what little information he knew, and Troy would be free to take care of the rest of his list.

The plan would work to perfection. If a murder and a diversion only cost him $100,000, it was well worth it.

Troy pulled his cap low over his eyes as he drove north on Front Street, heading for the house where he'd stored the materials he needed for the next phase of his plan.

As he cruised the narrow street, he reached down, turned on the radio, and tuned it to Philadelphia's all-news station. The sound of a Teletype and a man's baritone voice filled the car.

"Investigators in Cherry Hill, New Jersey, have linked the murder of a doorman in the Washington Commons Condominiums to this morning's ice-pick murders of Sharon Thomas and an unidentified man in North Philadelphia.

"Details are sketchy, but witnesses described seeing the suspect dressed in a workman's uniform and eyeglasses, leaving the scene of what turned out to be a grisly murder in the upscale building. Authorities are withholding the name of the victim until the next of kin can be notified, and they're asking that anyone with information about the suspect's whereabouts contact police immediately.

"KYW News Radio, the time is two fifty-two. Time for traffic and—"

Troy turned off the radio, took off the glasses he'd taken from

Mr. Williams, and pressed a little harder on the gas. This was no time for him to be out in the open.

If the police were his only concern, he could handle it. However, the general public now had his description, and he was more susceptible to delays.

As he gunned the engine to cross tiny Wishart Street, he missed the STOP sign, another car flew toward the intersection, and the loud screeching sound of skidding tires filled the air. They stopped just inches from one another.

The gray-haired driver released a long stream of curses in Spanish while shaking his fist out the window. Troy tipped his hat in apology and the old man cursed even louder.

When Troy pulled off, the man stopped cursing and stared at Troy with his mouth agape. Troy knew that he'd been recognized. He stomped the gas pedal into the floor and sped toward his next destination, leaving the old man staring helplessly as the car disappeared in the distance.

Troy glanced in his rearview mirror and saw that the old man's car hadn't moved. He was obviously in shock, having seen a murderer face-to-face.

There was nothing Troy could do about the old man seeing him. The best that Troy could hope for now was to avoid the same thing happening again.

It was time for him to move into the next phase of his plan. He pushed thoughts of the old man out of his mind, turned onto Allegheny Avenue, and drove toward the ramshackle apartment where he'd stored the equipment he needed.

He was just a few blocks from Kensington Avenue, in the notorious neighborhood known simply as K and A. It was a place where women sold themselves in darkness, desperately trying to find the means to pay for the drugs that sustained them. Men took what they could from the women in the hopes that they would somehow feel more like men. Neighbors stood helplessly by, victimized by it all, just as Troy believed that the city was victimized by women like Marilyn and Karima.

Yes, the apartment was the perfect place to start. The equipment he'd hidden under the creaky floorboards would give him what he needed to complete his list.

It was almost three o'clock now. He didn't have much time to get to Karima. Before he could go after her, Troy had to get to Marilyn. Just as he'd done with his father, he'd use the FBI to do it.

10.

Karima reached into her purse and gave her last two twenties to the driver who'd brought her to North Philly from Cherry Hill. Then she smiled sadly as she pondered the fact that the sheet of paper in her purse was worth far more than those last two bills.

She emerged from the cab on 26th and Oxford, and walked quickly toward the 26th Street speakeasy, a place she remembered from her time with Duane. Located just about two blocks from his corner, it was a place where high-end customers could rent rooms and smoke crack. It had never turned into a full-fledged crack house. The gamblers and drinkers wouldn't let it.

Beyond that, Karima didn't know much about the speakeasy. Rather than going in believing that the boy could show her where to find the killer, she walked toward the house carrying her purse, a Trio, and one other thing—hope.

That simple commodity was in short supply on a block where a few ramshackle houses stood quiet guard over nothing.

A stray cat crossed Karima's path. A woman crossed the street.

Karima crossed her fingers and hoped that the cops from Chuck's crime scene wouldn't see her as she walked up the steps to the house.

She kept her head down and knocked on the door. A few seconds later, a small metal plate slid back and a set of wizened eyes regarded her from inside. She heard a series of clicking locks, and then the door swung open.

"Where's the boy?" she asked as Mr. Vic waved her inside.

"Back here," he said, walking toward the back of the house with a briefcase in his hand.

Karima followed him through the dim passage, eyeing the old man's briefcase while gazing at the home's nineteenth-century woodwork and crumbling plaster.

As they walked the wide hallway, passing a living room and dining room before entering a small room off the kitchen, Karima could feel the misery that prevailed there. It was as palpable as the pain she'd felt from the time she'd seen her mother's blood pouring out on the courtroom floor.

Karima planned to make that pain go away by inflicting it on her mother's killer. As Mr. Vic led her into Skeet's room and placed the briefcase in the corner, she found a spot on the wall and stood with her back to it, warily watching them both.

"Thanks for comin'," Skeet said, looking from Karima to the old man. "I'm Skeet. This Mr. Vic. We—"

"Look, I don't have time for small talk," Karima said sharply. "I just need to get to the man who stabbed my mother before the police do."

Mr. Vic chimed in, "You talk about the cops like you not

workin' with 'em. I thought you was playin' both sides since you was out there with that captain from Homicide."

"Look, the only side I'm playing is mine," Karima said, sounding frustrated. "Now, if you can get me the man who killed my mother, I can make it worth your while. If not, stop wasting my time."

"We don't want your money," the old man said.

"Then what do you want?" Karima asked, sounding both confused and suspicious.

Mr. Vic opened his mouth to answer, but he was too slow.

"Okay, I'll tell you what *I* want," she said angrily. "I want the man who stabbed my mother to feel the same thing I feel right now. I want him to know what it's like to want to kill somebody so bad that it kills you on the inside. I want him to die just like my mother died this morning, and when he does, I want to be looking in his face. I want to see his face when his heart stops, so I know the exact moment when he busts hell wide open. He took away the only mother I had—a mother I never really got a chance to know. I'm going to kill him, and you're going to help me."

A tear rolled down her cheek as she slammed the palm of her hand against the wall. "Now tell me what you want!"

There was an awkward silence as they digested what she'd said. Mr. Vic looked at Skeet and saw that the boy was beginning to waver. Before he could jump in to stop him, Skeet had already begun to speak.

"I want a chance," the boy mumbled.

Karima thought she'd heard him wrong. "What did you say?"

"I said I want a chance."

"Don't listen to the boy, he—"

"Nah, Mr. Vic," Skeet said, as tears welled up in his eyes. "I can't."

Karima's rage had awakened something that Skeet didn't realize was there. As the boy reached up to wipe his tears with a hard, bitter swipe of his palm, the years of pent-up grief began to spill out.

"I can't do this," Skeet croaked, trying hard to maintain his composure.

"Do what?" Karima said.

"This!" Skeet shouted. He looked at the old man and spoke quietly. "Look, Mr. Vic, I'm sorry I got you into this, but I can't do this to her. Not now. Not with the way my mother died."

Skeet slumped his shoulders, and for the first time in years, he looked like the little boy who lived beneath the man-child's tough veneer.

Karima's rage softened, if only for a moment, because she saw in him the hurt and anger she saw in herself.

"How did she die?" she asked gently.

Skeet paused as blurry images from that night came back to him. "These dudes came in the bar where she worked and shot her," he said in a monotone, forcing himself to focus through grief that still felt fresh. "I don't remember a lot about it. I just remember how things changed after that."

Karima and the old man looked at one another as Skeet relived the carnage from that summer night when he was four. The tears in his eyes weren't caused by the memories of that night, they were spurred by the things that had haunted him on many nights afterward.

"I keep havin' this dream where I walk in the bar and see the man who pulled the trigger," he said as he stared into the past. "He sittin' there, havin' a drink with his homeys, while my mom layin' there bleedin'. They laughin' so hard they can't see me. In fact, nobody can see me. So I creep in real slow and walk up behind him and knock down his stool. All the sudden they stop laughin'. And the dude on the floor on his back, and I'm sittin' on his chest, and he lookin' up at me with that same scared look on his face that my mom musta had when he shot her.

"So I pull out this knife and I cut open his shirt. Then the whole bar start cheerin' while I cut a hole in his chest. Now this dude that was so tough when he shot my mom—this dude is cryin' and beggin' me to stop. But I can't stop. They won't let me stop. I stick the knife in as deep as I can. Then I reach in his chest and cut out his heart. When I look down . . ."

Skeet paused as the horror of his dreams filled his mind. "When I look down at his face," he said, his voice just barely a whisper, "the man that killed my mother look just like me."

The blood drained from Karima's face, because even though she was wide awake, she'd had that dream herself. As she contemplated what Skeet had said, she knew that she'd found the one person on earth who knew what she was feeling.

Compassion overtook her rage. Though her mind told her not to, her feet disobeyed, and she found herself walking slowly across the room.

The old man watched as she sat down on the cot and placed an arm around Skeet. The boy returned the gesture. Karima cried for the little girl she'd been, and Skeet cried for the boy he was, and together they grieved the mothers they'd lost.

For a moment, Karima felt like she'd finally met the brother she'd never had. At the thought of her brother, she realized why Skeet's dream had affected her so deeply.

"My mother's killer looks just like me, too," she said, getting up from the cot as Skeet and the old man watched her.

"Then you know who he is?" Mr. Vic asked.

"Yes," Karima said as she looked at him with tired eyes. "He's my brother. The same way he killed my mother, he's going to try to kill me."

Both Skeet and Mr. Vic were stunned. Neither of them knew what to say.

"I have to go," Karima said, moving toward the door.

"Wait," Skeet said, crossing the room and grabbing Karima by the arm.

She hesitated. Then she turned to him and waited.

"I wanna help you," he said earnestly.

Karima could see that he was sincere, but sincerity couldn't get her what she wanted.

"How can you help me when you don't know where he is?"

"We don't have to know," Mr. Vic said. "We know where *you* are. If you the one he want, all we gotta do is tell him where to find you. Then we wait for him to come to us."

"Why would you want to do that?"

"The same reason I was always gon' do it," the old man said, looking at Skeet with love in his eyes. "For him."

"I don't understand."

"You ain't s'posed to understand," Skeet said, looking around the dilapidated room. "You can't if you ain't never have to live in this."

"I was in the game for almost two years," Karima said defensively.

"Yeah, but you always had a choice. I never did. This where I live, Karima. Ain't a whole lotta options for me. That's why I went to work for Heads."

The hairs on the back of her neck stood up at the mention of Heads. She remembered seeing him in the neighborhood when Duane was alive. His eyes had always made her uncomfortable. More than once, she'd told Duane that Heads was an enemy just waiting to strike. Duane had never taken him seriously, not even when it was rumored that Heads was behind a bungled attempt on Duane's life.

The man Heads had hired to kill Duane was found dead in an alley the day after he shot at Duane and missed, but Heads had never paid a price for his alleged involvement. Karima didn't like Heads, and if Skeet worked for him, she knew she shouldn't like the boy, either.

"What do you do for Heads?" she asked as she stared at him intently.

Skeet looked at the watch he wore on his left wrist, then glanced at Mr. Vic with a troubled expression on his face.

"Usually I'm just a runner, but in a couple minutes, I'm supposed to tell him I'm bringin' you to meet him. He wanna pay you ten grand to tell him where to find the dude who killed Chuck and took his package this mornin'. That ain't all he want from you, though."

"I know that," Karima said, remembering the way his eyes had roamed her body when she'd seen him on the street months before.

"He wanna be a kingpin," Mr. Vic said. "He think if he kill this guy who took his shit this mornin', he'll be halfway to the place where Duane used to be. And if he get a woman like you, that'll take him the rest o' the way."

"What do you mean?" Karima asked.

"Look at you," Mr. Vic said, eyeing her expensive clutch, tailored clothes, and polished demeanor. "You got the one thing a man like Heads can never buy—class. You carry it with you everywhere you go, and if Heads had you on his arm, it would say somethin' words never could."

"That's why he want you, Karima," Skeet said earnestly. "Every hustler in Philly know who you is, and they all know they can't have you. So in Heads's mind, the only difference between bein' a hustler and bein' a kingpin . . . is you."

Karima knew they were right about Heads. She also knew that their plan was wrong. She wanted to give the boy a chance to start over as badly as Mr. Vic did, because Skeet was the only person she'd ever met who could possibly understand her rage. If they were going to do this, though, they needed to face the truth, so she gave it to them as plainly as she could.

"You'll never get the money you're looking for from Heads," she said without looking at either of them. "He's a small-time drug dealer who's lucky if he's got $20,000 to his name."

Skeet looked at Mr. Vic, as if waiting for him to rebut what Karima had said. Mr. Vic sighed and looked away from both of them. He knew Karima was right.

"We have to do it my way," she said, looking intently at the boy before regarding Mr. Vic with a confidence that was almost arrogant. "I can get whatever I want from Heads. When I do, you can get the money you need from me, but I'm going to need to talk to him."

The boy and the old man looked at one another, unsure of what to do. Before they could decide, Skeet's cell phone rang. They were out of time.

"Wuddup," Skeet said, looking up at Karima as Heads spoke. "Yeah, she right here."

Karima looked at Mr. Vic, who looked at Skeet and nodded.

The boy handed her the phone.

"This is Cream," she said smoothly.

"Where the guy at, Cream?" Heads said, pacing the floor of his girlfriend's condo while the blonde looked on with barely hidden jealousy.

"We'll get to that," Karima said easily. "I want some guarantees first."

"Ain't nothin' in life guaranteed, baby," he said sternly. "You should know that better than anybody."

Karima bristled. "You're wrong about that, because I can guarantee two things: you've never known a woman like me, and if you keep playing games, you never will."

"I ain't got time for no games," he said, matching her sharp tone with his own. "You bring me the man I want, we can do business."

He looked down at the blonde, who was sitting on the chaise longue and watching him as he crossed the room. "Maybe after we do business," he whispered into the phone, "we can do a little pleasure, too."

"What about the money?" Karima said bluntly.

"You need ten grand that bad? I thought your man left you better off than that."

"He did, and if you want to do anything beyond business, you need to show me that you can do the same thing."

"So what you sayin'?"

"I'm saying I need to know you can handle yours," she said, her tone deadly serious. "If I bring you the man you want, I need to know that you're going to take care of him."

"I will."

"As far as the money goes, you can keep the ten grand."

"Why?"

"Because I want to see *fifty* grand. If you can't show me that, you can't keep up with me, and I can't put up the money it'll take to get you to the next level."

"I don't need you to take me to the next level," Heads said, growing angry.

"Maybe you don't," she said calmly. "But I don't need you, either. I've got my own money, and wherever I invest myself, that's where the money goes, too. The question is, are you worth the investment?"

Heads wasn't quite sure what to say. He'd never taken the time to think beyond the moment.

"I can bring you the man you want in less than an hour," she said, knowing she'd gotten his attention. "When I do, be prepared to show me the money. Now, where do you want to meet?"

There was a long moment of silence on the phone as Heads looked at the blonde, who cost him more than ten thousand dollars a month, and compared the burden of keeping her to the prospect of building with Cream.

The decision wasn't a difficult one.

"The old factory at 20th and Clearfield," he said. "I'll see you there in forty-five minutes, and I'll have the money."

Kevin Lynch drove back from Cherry Hill, New Jersey, his mind reeling with thoughts of the danger that Karima had placed herself in by leaving.

He knew that Troy Williams wouldn't stop until he or his sister was dead. He knew that his detectives had found the book at Marilyn's house, and that the connection he'd seen between Jansen and Marilyn in the courtroom had been confirmed.

As righteous as he'd felt in judging the FBI agent's fawning behavior toward Marilyn, he now felt foolish when he thought about his own actions with Karima.

The commissioner had seen it. No doubt, others had as well. For the first time in his career, he wasn't sure if the case before him was the most important thing in his life.

He crossed the Ben Franklin Bridge and made his way into Philadelphia, crossing an emotional bridge as well. Rather than making a left on 8th Street and heading to police headquarters, he turned on his dome lights and drove straight toward the only real emergency in his life.

Moving from the east side of the city to the west, he drew closer to the place where he needed to be, and his mind was overtaken by the memories that had brought him to this moment.

He recalled the day his daughter was born—the way she'd opened her eyes and looked around the delivery room as if she'd seen it all before. He remembered the way she'd snatched the microphone away from the other children the first time she sang in the youth choir at their church. Her first day of kindergarten and the way she'd stood in line—the only child to do so without tears. Her first date, and the way he'd intimidated the boy by cleaning his gun in the living room. Lynch smiled at the memories. Then he parked the car and hoped that he hadn't squandered his chance to create more.

The freshman orientation was taking place at College Hall, near 34th and Walnut Streets. Though it was almost over for everyone else, it was just beginning for Lynch.

He ran up the steps and into the building, flashing his badge for the security guard. Then he ran up to the second floor and squeezed into the room where the rest of the parents and their children had gathered.

As he made his way farther in, he felt out of place, just as he always did in those kinds of settings. He wasn't accustomed to the niceties that everyone else engaged in. The fake smiles, innocuous small talk, and furtive glances were foreign to him. He was used to the rough-and-tumble world of policing, where the communication was real and the interaction basic.

Fortunately, he didn't have to speak. By the time he made his way to the middle of the standing room only crowd, the president of the university was already up at the podium. She seemed to be speaking directly to Kevin Lynch.

"And to the parents of these young people," she said, her tone earnest. "Know that you already have so much to be proud of. They wouldn't have made it without your love, your guidance, and your influence. If you hadn't placed the highest expectations on them, they wouldn't have risen to meet them. So as we welcome these young people to the next phase of their lives, we owe you a debt of gratitude, because without you, they wouldn't be here.

"Please enjoy the food our staff has prepared for you, enjoy the tour of the university, and enjoy your children. Treasure this moment, because you'll never have a chance to share this day with them again."

The room erupted in applause, and as the president moved off to the side to greet the various VIPs who had come to pay tribute to the city's largest employer, the other attendees moved toward the food serving stations that had been set up on the far side of the room.

Lynch wasn't interested in the food. Nor was he curious about the VIPs. He wanted to see his family, so he scanned the crowd in the hopes of spotting Jocelyn and Chantal.

It didn't take him long to find them.

With a mumbled "Excuse me," he began moving toward the line that had formed at the hand-carved beef Wellington station. He could see Jocelyn's brown dreadlocks standing out among the blond and brunette hairstyles surrounding her. As he got closer, he could see Chantal leaning against her mother's shoulder. Her face was obscured, but Lynch knew that the expression she wore reflected something other than the happiness she should have felt.

More than that, though, he knew it was his fault.

"Hi," he said simply, as he sidled up to them.

Chantal's face lit up. "Daddy!" she shouted, leaving her mother's shoulder and leaping into her father's arms.

"Hello," Jocelyn said, arching a single eyebrow in lieu of asking the questions that were running through her mind.

"Can I talk to you?" Lynch said, looking from Jocelyn to his daughter. "Both of you?"

Jocelyn wanted to curse him. She wanted to embarrass him. But she had never been one to cause a scene in public, and she wasn't planning to do so now.

"Sure," she said with a fake smile. "Why don't you and Chantal grab a table and I'll get us some food. I'll be over in a minute."

Lynch nodded as his wife's smile disappeared. Then he put his arm around his daughter's shoulder and walked her across the cavernous room.

"I'm proud of you, honey," he said with all the sincerity he could muster.

"I know," she said, leaning against her father.

Lynch stopped walking, took her by both shoulders, and held her at arm's length. "How do you know?" he said, looking her in the eye.

"I just do," she said, avoiding her father's probing stare.

Lynch knew then that everything his wife had said was right. He hadn't been there for either of them the way they needed him to. For years, he had left them to assume what he felt for them. They deserved a lot more than that.

"Chantal, I know you heard your mother and me arguing this morning." He chuckled. "I know you've heard us arguing a lot of mornings, evenings, nights, weekends."

Chantal grinned in spite of herself. "Isn't that what marriage is all about?"

"Not when you're doing it right," he said soberly. "And I haven't done it right. Not for a long time. I haven't done fatherhood right, either."

"Dad, you've been a great father. You've just got a demanding career, that's all. I understand."

"You shouldn't have to understand," he said earnestly. "You shouldn't have to guess. You should know that I'm proud of you, because I should tell you every day just how lucky I am to have you for a daughter. You should know that I love you because I should tell you out of my own mouth every day. I don't, and I have to change."

Chantal reached out to hug him, and tears stung his eyes as he melted into her embrace. He felt like a fool for being so willing to throw all this away.

As Lynch and his daughter rocked back and forth holding each other, Jocelyn approached Lynch from behind with plates of food in her hands. He couldn't hear her footsteps above the din of thousands of people speaking at once. Jocelyn could hear him, though. He spoke to Chantal, and it almost seemed that he was speaking to her.

"I almost didn't come today," Lynch said, disengaging from their embrace and looking around the room. "I almost put my work before my family again. I'm glad I didn't. Looking at you now, I see that you're just as beautiful as your mother was on the first day I saw her on this campus. You've got that same intelligence, that same curiosity, that same fierceness in your spirit."

He took his daughter's face in his hands. "They say the best thing you get out of college is your degree," he said, looking at her with a loving smile. "But the best thing I took from here was her. She gave me everything I'd ever dreamed of in a woman, and as a bonus, she gave me you."

Lynch reached up and wiped his eyes, then looked around

self-consciously. "Maybe someday, when we're able to talk again, I'll tell her that."

"I think you just did," Chantal said, looking over his shoulder and smiling at her mother.

Lynch turned around and saw his wife. She was standing there with her mouth open, unsure of what to believe until she looked in his eyes.

There, she saw an apology for the years of neglect. She saw the regret for what he had done. She saw a willingness to change.

The plates clattered to the floor and the room fell silent as Jocelyn rushed into her husband's arms. The two of them stood in the middle of the room, embracing for the world to see. Jocelyn realized that she had done exactly what she'd promised herself she wouldn't. She'd caused a scene.

"I'm sorry," Lynch whispered in his wife's ear. "I took you for granted. I neglected our family."

"Kevin, don't—"

"No, Jocelyn, I was wrong," he said, leaning back and looking her in the eye. "I was wrong to do it, wrong to defend it, and even more wrong to try to put the blame on you. You're the one who looked out for us when I was busy looking out for me. I know I can't change everything overnight, but I'm willing to try."

He pulled his wife close. "I only hope you're willing to let me."

Jocelyn searched his eyes as everyone in the room willed her to respond. A moment stretched into two as she looked at her daughter, as if to request her approval.

Chantal smiled and nodded slightly, and Jocelyn reached up to hug her husband tightly. As he lifted her off the floor, the weight of too many empty years was lifted off her shoulders.

The two of them hugged for what seemed an eternity. Chantal wrapped her arms around her parents, while the other people in the room began to clap. They saw the love that filled that tight circle, a love that had been tested more than they knew.

As Lynch stood there with his family, he was simply a father and husband, a man whose life revolved around the people with whom he shared it. He felt his wife's soft maturity in his arms. He felt the tender touch of his daughter's hands. He felt like he could stay there with them forever.

Then, just as a maintenance worker came to clean up the broken plates and the other families went back to their own private joy, Lynch's BlackBerry began to vibrate. Reality broke into their celebration.

Jocelyn and Chantal released him and waited to see what he would do. When he didn't answer, his wife smiled.

"You can't run from them any more than you can run from us," she said, touching his cheek.

"I know," Lynch said. "But this is our time. They'll just have to wait."

"They can't," Jocelyn said. "They need you."

"I thought—"

She put a finger against his lips. "There's nothing to think about," his wife said. "Not with a man running around the city killing people. You're a Homicide captain. You belong out there finding that killer. After you do that, we want you to do one thing for us."

"Come home," Chantal said, completing her mother's thought.

Lynch looked at them both as if he were seeing them for the very first time. Then he hugged his wife and daughter once again, gazed up at the hallowed halls of his alma mater, and slipped out of the room to do what he did best—find a killer.

The lights atop the black Ford Taurus blazed red and blue as Special Agent John Kowalski sped toward the Philadelphia Federal Detention Center with Marilyn Johnson in tow.

A call from headquarters had just confirmed his worst fears. When federal agents went to interview the elderly couple who'd adopted Troy as a boy, they found that Troy had gotten to Elton and Mamie Williams first.

One thing was clear. Troy Williams was systematically eliminating people from his past. So far, the authorities knew about five victims. Kowalski only hoped that he could get to Bill Johnson before the body count rose to six.

He pulled up in back of the prison, flashed his badge, and was waved through the massive electric door that led to the prisoners' entrance.

As the door closed behind them, he could see that the normal order of the FDC had been replaced by controlled chaos. Two ambulances were parked in the bay, their lights spinning as a bevy of prison guards, administrators, and paramedics milled about.

Kowalski jumped out of the car with Marilyn close behind him. A second later, two more paramedics emerged from the prison with an inmate on a gurney. One of them was furiously pumping the inmate's chest in an effort to revive him. The other was guiding the wheeled stretcher into the back of the ambulance.

Kowalski pressed closer and Marilyn reluctantly followed. When they reached the back of the ambulance, the man's face was clearly visible. Marilyn gasped when she saw her husband. Like everyone within ten feet of him, she could see that Bill Johnson was dead.

The paramedic who'd been doing CPR stopped pumping his chest. The other grabbed a sheet and started to cover the body. Kowalski held a hand up to stop him.

"Mrs. Johnson?" he said, turning to Marilyn. "Is this your husband?"

She broke down in tears. Then she mumbled a barely audible "Yes" as Kowalski looked at her with disdain.

He nodded to the paramedic, who covered him with a sheet. Then he looked at Marilyn and judged her tears to be meaningless in the face of what she'd just done with Jansen.

The warden, who'd stood there with his guards and administrators as Bill Johnson was wheeled out of the prison, instructed the paramedics to take the body back inside to be processed.

Kowalski approached the warden with his badge on display. "Special Agent John Kowalski."

"Frank Green," the warden said, shaking Kowalski's proffered hand.

"How long ago did you find Mr. Johnson?"

"We found him a little after three. Obviously, there was nothing we could do."

"Who was the last guard to have contact with him?"

"One of our sharpest guys. Name's Reed. Josh Reed. His shift ended at three o'clock, but he should be on his way back now to file a report. He—"

"You have a cell number for him?" Kowalski said, interrupting him.

"Yes, but I don't understand why that's significant. He should be on his way back."

"I need someone to get me his cell number," Kowalski said, his tone just shy of frantic.

"Why?"

"Because that guard had something to do with Mr. Johnson's death."

"That's not possible," the warden said, sounding defensive. "Every inch of this facility is monitored."

"I'm not saying you're responsible for this, but if you don't help us find out what Reed knows about the five murders connected to this one, you might be responsible for whatever happens next."

The warden hesitated ever so slightly. Then he dialed Personnel on his BlackBerry, got Reed's cell phone number, and gave it to Kowalski.

"Thanks," the agent said, grabbing Marilyn and hustling her to the car.

Quickly, he backed onto the street as the door to the bay opened, then grabbed his cell phone and dialed headquarters.

He hoped he wasn't too late.

11.

Troy backed the car into an abandoned lot on tiny Shelbourne Street, threw dirt and leaves on the hood to camouflage it, then walked past a group of children as he made his way to Kensington and Allegheny.

He knew he didn't have much time. Then again, Troy was accustomed to doing things in a hurry. Scrambling up the stairs of the three-story building where he'd rented a studio apartment weeks before, he took a shiny key from his pocket and opened the door.

When he walked inside, the place looked exactly as he remembered it. The walls bore the telltale signs of neglect, and the tattered shades barely covered the windows. There was no furniture except for the plastic milk crates he'd brought with him on the day he'd handed three months' rent to the slumlord who owned the building. Above the kitchen sink, there was a cracked mirror. Below it, there was a worn transistor radio and rusted pipes.

Troy wasn't there for the amenities. He was there to go forward with his plan, come hell or high water.

He locked the door behind him and looked out the front and back windows to see if anything on the streets appeared to be out of place. In back of the building, there was the same emptiness that had always been there. In front of the building, K and A looked the same as it had when he'd decided to use this place as the staging area for the final phase of his plan.

Seeing it again was a relief, because he'd almost forgotten how perfect it was.

K and A was a bustling commercial strip whose business enterprises ran the gamut from legal to illegal, and everything in between. There were heroin addicts whose plodding movements were the opposite of the quick, gyrating motions of crack prostitutes. There were electronics stores whose Israeli and Arab owners found common ground in their willingness to fence stolen merchandise. There were drug dealers locked in a constant, dangerous dance with the cops and one another. In the midst of it all, there was the Catholic mission whose meals gave steaming bowls of hope to the denizens of the wretched strip.

All of it worked to form an uneasy balance. It was the reason that Troy had chosen to operate from this place. The bad and the good coexisted here, and while he had no illusion about the evil of his means, Troy believed that they were justified by the ends.

He still remembered the day he realized what he'd been born to do. It was three years before, during one of his first cases with the Bureau.

Troy and his assistant were cross-checking public records to compile a list of suspects in the shooting of an undercover FBI agent.

"Take a look at this," Troy's assistant said, holding open a folder for Troy to review. "This guy was adopted by a Mr. and Mrs. Elton Williams. Looks like he might've been removed from the home, and . . ."

Troy's blood ran cold at the mention of his foster parents, and Josh's voice faded into the background. Troy hadn't thought of his childhood since abandoning an attempt at therapy during college. Since then, he'd hidden his simmering rage, preferring to pour his fury into marathon workouts at the gym.

As Josh continued to talk, Mr. Williams's name flashed across Troy's mind like a movie credit, and the film of Troy's last beating began to play. He felt the lash of the belt against his back, the pounding of fists against his ribs, and the sound of Chuck and Mrs. Williams laughing in the basement. The memories caused tears to stream down Troy's cheeks, and rage to bubble up inside him.

"Are you all right?" Josh asked, breaking into Troy's thoughts.

Troy quickly wiped his face and pasted on an uncomfortable smile. "I guess I've been looking at this stuff too long," he said nervously. "My eyes are watering."

Josh nodded slowly, but he wasn't convinced. He was concerned about Troy.

"Take a break," Troy said, taking the folder before Josh could ask any questions. "I'll look into this and see if we can find out where this guy went after foster care."

In the days that followed, Troy learned that the Williams family had been barred from providing foster care after abusing five different boys. They avoided criminal charges by claiming that Mr. Williams suffered from mental illness.

After Troy learned that he could use his FBI credentials to get confidential information on children given up for adoption, he made the call that would forever change his life.

"This is Josh Reed," Troy said, anxiously looking behind him to make sure his assistant didn't come into the room. "I'm with the FBI, and we're working on a murder case. We need some information on a Mr. Troy Williams, birth date January 15, 1983. He was fostered by Mr. and Mrs. Elton Williams in the early '90s. I need to know his birth mother's name."

Troy's heart raced as the woman told him to hold on. When she came back on the line and gave him Sharon's name, Troy's hands began to shake.

"Thank you," he croaked as he hung up the phone.

When he turned around, Josh was standing in the doorway, staring at him. The look on his face said that he'd heard almost everything.

"I-I just needed to know," Troy said nervously. "I'm sorry I used your name. I hope you understand."

They both knew that Troy could face criminal charges for obtaining confidential information that way.

"No," Josh said, closing the door behind him and taking a seat. "I don't understand. Why don't you explain?"

For hours, Troy sat down with Josh, telling him everything he could remember about his childhood. Troy cried when he recalled the beatings, the rejection, and the fear.

Seeing this hulking, brilliant man whom he admired reduced to tears stirred something in Josh, who'd spent most of his life as an outsider—ignored and often mocked as a nerd.

"How can I help you find out more about your family?" Josh asked. "I mean, if you know who they are, maybe you can put it behind you."

That question began a three-year odyssey that led to the discovery of Troy's affluent roots and his mother's troubled past. When the Tatum case came along and Troy was assigned the task of researching the Thomas family, the floodgates opened.

Instead of healing him from the hurt, the intimate knowledge crystallized Troy's hatred. The more he learned about them, the angrier he became.

"They ruined my life before it could even begin," he told Josh on the day he decided to leave the Bureau. "My mother's a whore who slept with her sister's husband. My father's a coward who was too afraid to leave his wife, and Marilyn is a power-hungry bitch who was willing to ruin all of us just to hold on to a man she didn't love."

Troy's eyes filled with unspeakable hate. "I want them all dead," Troy said as Josh looked at him with a shocked expression. "Right down to the twin who lived the life I should've had."

For a week, Josh considered turning Troy in, but when they discovered Duane's money and Troy offered to pay Josh $100,000 to help, things changed.

Now, three years after stumbling across a gateway to his past, Troy marveled at himself for having plotted his revenge and carried it out so well.

As he stood in the ramshackle apartment and scanned the

names from his list, he knew that he only had two people left: Marilyn and Karima.

Troy walked to the corner of the room and pried open the floorboards where he'd hidden the tools he would need to complete his plan.

When he opened them, he smiled, because everything he'd put there was still in place, waiting to be used. On top was a pair of jeans, sneakers, a 76ers cap, a fake beard, and a size 5X T-shirt. Beneath that was a backpack containing a forty-caliber semiautomatic handgun and enough rounds of ammunition to supply a small army. There were a set of keys to the Chevy. On the bottom, there were the most important objects of all: a laptop with a wireless PCS connection card and global positioning software, a cell phone, and $20,000 in cash.

Troy stripped to his underwear and removed the items from beneath the floorboards. Quickly, he put on the outfit and placed the gun in his waistband. Then he took out the laptop, scurried to the corner of the room and set the computer atop a crate.

"Thank God for the FBI," he mumbled as he turned on the laptop, inserted the PCS connection card, and activated the GPS software he'd pirated from the Bureau.

Thanks to the extensive research he'd done on his birth family while working on the Tatum murder case, he had every piece of vital information on Marilyn and Karima, including Social Security numbers, bank account numbers, passwords, and cell phone numbers. He would use only a portion of that information to finish what he'd begun.

He typed in a user name and password in order to access the

software, and in minutes he was tracking his prey with keystrokes rather than hounds. The footprints were left by the GPS chips that were installed in the high-end cell phones that both Marilyn and Karima carried. The scent they left behind was followed by satellites and routing towers.

Punching in Marilyn's cell phone number, he watched as the system used triangulation technology to find the location of Marilyn's phone. In less than a minute, the system determined that she was close to 6th and Market, which led Troy to believe that she was near the James Byrne Federal Building. With a few more keystrokes, he learned that her last location had been less than a block away, at 7th and Arch, and that it had taken her a mere three minutes to travel from one point to the other.

Troy smiled, because the system had confirmed what he already suspected. Marilyn had been to the prison to identify her husband's body. Now she was apparently in one of the two new cars the FBI had been using to transport federal witnesses in Philadelphia.

Troy knew that both specially equipped vehicles had been outfitted with bulletproof glass at Quantico, Virginia. During his last week with the Bureau, Troy had outfitted them with something else as well: cell phones.

It had taken a little more than a minute to attach the modified phones to the gas tanks on the undersides of the cars. It would take even less time to dial the numbers and turn them into triggering devices.

As he used the GPS system to track Marilyn's progress on the computer, Troy wondered if the walls of the prison had unnerved her. He wondered if the sight of Bill Johnson's corpse had frightened her. He wondered which of the agents was accompanying her.

Most of all, he wondered if she knew she was next.

"Just find him!" Kowalski screamed into his cell phone for the third time.

He was aggravated—and not only because they'd been stuck in traffic for two minutes. He was angry because he'd been on his cell phone for at least that long asking an FBI surveillance team to track Josh Reed, and they kept talking about paperwork.

"Look, I'll get to the paperwork!" he shouted in frustration. "I need you to hear me. Josh Reed just killed a federal witness in the FDC and he's working with another killer. If we get to Reed, we get them both. Now get Reed's picture to every airport, train station, and bus station on the East Coast, and get some agents to grab him before someone else dies."

Kowalski disconnected the call as the traffic cleared. He whipped around the cars that had blocked their path and skidded onto 8th Street. Turning on his police lights, he darted quickly through the clogged traffic.

"Mrs. Johnson, I'll be frank," Kowalski said angrily. "I don't like you, and after that shit you pulled with Jansen today, I don't trust you, either. But I need to know why these murders are happening, and I need to know now."

"How am I supposed to know?"

"Because you had your father's little black book. You knew Sharon had two babies, and you knew she put one of them up for adoption."

"I didn't know that," Marilyn said, trying and failing to sound innocent. "I never even looked at my father's book."

"That's a lie. If you don't stop telling lies, you're going to die."

Marilyn didn't respond, though his words echoed in her mind, frightening her.

Kowalski skidded onto Market Street, sped toward 6th, and hung a U-turn at almost fifty miles per hour, the tires of the car kicking up white smoke as he screeched to a halt in front of the Federal Building.

When he stopped, Marilyn opened the door and tried to get out.

Kowalski reached over her and slammed it shut. "New rules," he said with authority. "You don't move until I tell you to. You don't go anywhere without me. And you don't speak to anyone unless I've spoken to them first. Understand?"

A federal security officer came over to the car. Before he could ask them to move, Kowalski lowered Marilyn's window and flashed his badge. The security officer backed away and Kowalski closed the window.

"Why are you treating me like this?" Marilyn said in a tone that was almost meek.

"Because you're a target!" he said sharply. "It was one thing when you were just a witness against greedy politicians. Things are different now. Troy Williams is obviously determined to kill specific people. And I think you may be one of them."

"You're crazy," Marilyn said dismissively.

"No, *he's* crazy. In less than twenty-four hours, he's killed his mother, his father, his foster parents, and the only man he could've considered a brother."

"Yes, but why would he want to kill me?" she said, laughing nervously. "It's like you said. He's crazy."

"You really don't know what you're dealing with, do you?" he asked in a condescending tone. "Troy worked for the FBI. He helped us figure out killers. So nothing he's doing is random. And he's not going to do it by the book. Now, if you want to play games with me or with Jansen, that might cost you some freedom. If you play games with this guy, it just might cost you your life."

Marilyn looked at Kowalski and saw that he was serious. She looked at herself and understood that she was trapped. It was then that she knew that she could no longer manipulate her circumstances. Neither her brain nor her beauty could change the madness that was brewing in Troy's mind. He was acting on a chain of events that had begun long before his birth, and he wouldn't stop until he'd achieved his goal.

"What do you want to know?" she asked quietly.

"I want to know the significance of that book we found at your house. Is there anything there that can tell us why he's doing this? More importantly, is there anything there that can tell us how to make him stop?"

Marilyn took a deep breath and thought back to her family's deepest secrets. Though she'd never believed that she would tell them, she knew that now was the time to let them go.

"The book was just a way for an old politician to control people," she said quietly. "What you really want to know about is Troy, and there's only one thing I can tell you about him: he's not the first one in our family to do something like this."

Marilyn took a deep breath. "Back in Camden, South

Carolina—where my family's from originally—there were a couple of scandals in the thirties and early forties. The first one was about my grandmother. She used to hear voices. Those voices would tell her to kill people, but Grandma wasn't willing to do that. Eventually, she hung herself. Granddaddy remarried, and for a while, everything was fine. But when my father was about thirteen, they found seven members of his family dead in a shack on the back road where they lived.

"Turned out my father's older brother, George—my grandmother's first son—decided one day that he needed to kill everyone in the house. Thank God my father was spending the summer here in Philadelphia, or he would have died, too. As it was, George killed everyone else in less than twenty minutes. The only person he missed was the one he really wanted—his twin sister, Georgia.

"By the time my cousins heard about it and made it out to the house, my Uncle George was holed up in an upstairs bedroom with a shotgun, and Georgia was hiding downstairs in the basement.

"A couple hours went by and every time they tried to convince him to come out, he kept yelling, 'Get me Georgia! This ain't over 'til I get Georgia!'

"Eventually, she came up out of the basement and went into that bedroom to try to reason with him. A few minutes later, there were two shotgun blasts: one for her and one for him.

"Over the years, as my father became more prominent, he fixed it so the people down there would say the Klan did it. That way, his political opponents couldn't use it against him. Truth is, we always knew that George was insane. From everything they told me about him and my grandmother, it sounded like they had some kind of hereditary mental illness. We think it was paranoid schizophrenia. I guess that's why I never had children. I was afraid that I would pass it down to them."

Marilyn looked the agent in the eye for the first time since she'd begun telling the story.

"George was a lot like Troy. His mind was so sharp that he couldn't stand the burden of his intellect. And he blamed everyone else for that—especially his twin.

"If you want to know how you can stop Troy," she said, her tone grave, "you really only have one hope: get to his twin before he does."

Kowalski was silent as he digested the information. The two of them were contemplating the meaning of the madness that had plagued the Thomas family for generations when the muffled sound of a ringing cell phone penetrated their thoughts. They looked at each other, bewildered. Neither of their cell phones was ringing. Kowalski was about to dismiss it as nothing. Then he remembered that cell phones could be used to set off bombs.

A second before Troy's phone call triggered the reaction between the explosives and the gas tank, Kowalski opened the car door and tried to push Marilyn out.

The blast that followed blew her into the side of the James Byrne Federal Building. It disintegrated most of Agent Kowalski's right side. It obliterated the vehicle. And as pieces of hot metal sprinkled down on the street like black rain, Marilyn Johnson died on the sidewalk.

Troy's victim list was whittled down to one.

* * *

Karima, the old man, and the boy sat in Mr. Vic's old Cadillac on Clearfield Street, staring at the factory where the meeting with Heads would take place.

At Karima's insistence, they'd arrived nearly thirty minutes early, and they'd come with three different sets of hopes. Skeet sat in the back seat, hoping that Heads would show up with the money Karima had demanded to see. If he did, the boy wouldn't have to wait for Karima to fund his escape from the life he despised. Heads would do it for her. Mr. Vic, who sat in the driver's seat, was more circumspect. He'd seen plans go wrong before. His hope was that things would be different this time. But without using the contents of the briefcase he'd placed on the car's back seat, he was almost powerless to make it happen. Karima, who sat in the passenger seat, stared out the window at the rusty water towers, abandoned factories, ramshackle houses, and lost dreams. She wondered if her dream of avenging her mother could come true in such a place. She wondered if she really wanted it to.

Karima glanced at Skeet, and saw that his expression, like the old man's, was intense. He was focused on changing his life. He should've been. It was he who had the most to lose. The old man had lived his life, and Karima had lived more in twenty-three years than most people do in a hundred.

As they sat on the pothole-ridden street, inhaling the stench of garbage and waist-high weeds from the gated, blocklong lot to their right, Karima realized that their lives weren't over. In fact, they were just beginning. If anyone's life was going to be put in jeopardy for this, it should be hers.

"I don't know if the two of you want to stay here," she said, looking from Skeet to Mr. Vic. "Things might not go the way we planned, and—"

"Plans don't never go like they s'posed to," Mr. Vic said, interrupting her. "That's why I brought these."

He leaned back, reached over the driver's seat for the briefcase, sat it on his lap, and opened it. There were three nine-millimeters and ten full clips inside.

"You know you don't have to do this," Karima said to the old man, as if giving him another chance to back out would make a difference.

"Take this gun," he said firmly. Then he reached into the briefcase and held it in his hand.

Karima looked at him with gratitude in her eyes. Then she took it, checked the chamber, and slapped a clip into place. Skeet reached over the back seat and did the same.

Mr. Vic took the third gun and loaded it as he spoke. "I ain't come out here to leave y'all alone," he said as he examined the gun. "I came out here to make things right—for Skeet's mother, for your mother, and for me."

He paused for a moment and stared into his past. "I did a lotta shit in my life that I ain't proud of," he said softly. "But if we do this—if we get the man who killed your mother, and get Skeet outta this bullshit—I'll know when I die that I did at least one thing right."

The three of them looked at each other with a mixture of fear and camaraderie. Then Karima reached into her purse and extracted her Trio.

"When I do this, my brother's coming," she said, turning around to look at Skeet. "And there won't be any turning back."

The boy nodded, urging her to do what she must.

With one last glance at Mr. Vic, she took out the piece of paper Duane had given her, logged on to the Internet from her phone, and accessed the offshore account.

Her fingers shaking, she entered the numbers that Duane had provided her. The page took what seemed like an eternity to load.

"Here it is," Karima said as the account information showed up on the screen.

She saw that there was only $400,000 in the account. That meant that Troy had already accessed it.

As Skeet and Mr. Vic watched, Karima pushed a few buttons and initiated a wire transfer. The money would move to another account soon, and Troy would use the same tools that the Feds used to track her down.

"He's coming," she said, putting the phone away.

As the three of them sat in silence, waiting for Troy and Heads to show up, they heard the happy sounds of bass-heavy music and children playing, old men laughing and young men shouting. They could hear the sounds of life in a section of North Philly where the factories had died long ago.

Then, somewhere farther off, they heard the echo of hundreds of sirens wailing in unison. Whatever had happened was big enough to elicit responses from every emergency vehicle in Philadelphia.

In her heart, Karima knew that it was somehow connected to Troy.

The explosion had rocked everything within a one-mile radius of the Federal Building, including Philadelphia Police Headquarters, which was barely four blocks away.

In seconds, rumors of a terrorist attack swept through Center City.

FBI agents and U.S. marshals blocked access to the federal building. Park rangers closed Independence National Historical Park. Transit police shut down the subway system. Thousands of workers were evacuated from office buildings, including City Hall.

As bedlam reigned outside, Police Headquarters—and especially the police radio room—was strained to the breaking point. Troy Williams's killing spree had already generated hundreds of calls, and after the suspected terrorist attack on the federal building, the calls were coming in by the thousands.

"Police radio, operator five-two," a veteran call-taker said as she took her tenth call in succession.

"I think I saw the man who stabbed the lady in the courtroom," said an old man with a thick Spanish accent.

The operator sighed. She'd been getting these kinds of calls all day. Half of them were from nuts. The other half were from well-meaning citizens who couldn't identify their next-door neighbors if they had to.

"Where did you see him, sir?" she asked with a sigh.

"Front Street, near Wishart, about half a block from Allegheny. He ran a STOP sign and almost hit my car."

She dutifully typed in the location on her computer and asked the obligatory question.

"What did he look like?"

"He had light brown skin and he had on green work clothes with glasses and a cap."

"Any other distinguishing characteristics?"

"He was driving a new red Buick. I can't say the name. Lu-something."

The call-taker looked up from her computer screen as a chill ran through her body. The mention of the car had awakened her, because a red Buick Lucerne had been reported missing from City Hall about an hour before. Its owner, Regina Brown, was missing, too.

"Do you have a license plate number?" she asked as she stood up in her cubicle and waved to get her supervisor's attention.

"I do," the caller said. "Hold on a minute."

The call-taker heard papers rustling as he searched for the plate number.

"It's KRS8458," he said as she scribbled the number on a piece of scrap paper and handed it to the supervisor.

Covering the small microphone on her headset, she whispered so the caller couldn't hear.

"I'm sending the information back to the dispatchers. Can you make sure they run the plate right now?"

"In case you haven't heard, there's been an attack on the federal building," the corporal said sarcastically. "They'll run it when they get a chance."

The call-taker rolled her eyes. She hated dealing with this corporal. He was one of the new breed of uniformed supervisors who'd been transferred from patrol to the radio room. The call-taker had been there for over twenty years. She wasn't about to be questioned by someone who'd only been there for two.

"This caller saw Troy Williams driving the chief clerk's missing car," she said with an attitude. "Now, you can take my word for it and have them run the plate, or you can play games and get the city sued for mishandling this call. It's up to you."

The corporal started to argue, but he'd heard about lawsuits based on bungled 9-1-1 calls before. He didn't want his name mixed up in one, so he took the sheet of paper to the dispatchers and had them run the plate.

The call-taker got back on the phone and pressed the old man for more information. "Sir, how long ago did you see him, and which way was he going?"

"I saw him maybe fifteen minutes ago. I started arguing with him 'cause he almost hit my car, but—"

"Which way did he go, sir? Do you remember?"

"He made a right on Allegheny from Front Street. I'm not sure where he went from there."

The call-taker finished typing in the information, labeled the call a robbery in progress, and pushed the SEND button. The dispatchers handling East Division got the call. Having already run the plate at the corporal's behest, they knew that the call might be legitimate. The car did indeed belong to Regina Brown.

They still weren't sure that Troy Williams was the driver, but the description was the same one they'd been broadcasting for the last hour. With the license plate coming up registered to a missing person, there was a chance this was a solid lead.

While the police department's Central Division was mired down with the explosion at the federal building, East Division had the personnel to handle the search for Troy Williams. Though they were stretched thin, the radio room did, too.

A sergeant rushed up to join the veteran dispatchers working

East Band. A lieutenant joined them soon afterward, but the dispatchers already knew what to do. The supervisors had only to watch.

The alert tone sounded, and seconds later, the call went out over every band in the city.

"Cars stand by. Flash information on Troy Williams, suspect in multiple stabbings in Philadelphia. He was spotted fifteen minutes ago in the vicinity of Front and Allegheny wearing a green work uniform, glasses, and cap, and driving a red Buick Lucerne with a Pennsylvania license tag of KRS8458. Use caution, that car is registered to Regina Brown, who was reported missing from City Hall this afternoon. Williams was last seen traveling east on Allegheny from Front Street fifteen minutes ago."

The radio came to life as every officer in the Twenty-fourth District responded. In mere minutes, dispatchers and supervisors divided Allegheny Avenue and the surrounding streets into sectors. Each car was given four blocks to patrol. The lieutenant working the streets oversaw the search. The two sergeants rode the length of Allegheny Avenue from Front to Kensington to double-check the areas that had been assigned to the patrol officers.

Central Division didn't have any patrol officers left, so they sent two officers who normally worked in the Ninth District Captain's office to check Regina's home. Not five minutes went by before they delivered their grim news.

"Nine-Tom Two, we're on location," the sergeant said. "We got word from the neighbors that they'd heard some noises coming from the house. We entered the garage."

There was a pause as the officer composed himself.

"Send Rescue," he said somberly. "Just have them use caution. We've got a 5292 here."

The dispatchers knew what that meant. Regina Brown was dead. Her car was gone, and as the minutes ticked by, it became more apparent that the man who'd been spotted driving it on the other side of town was Troy Williams.

Police radio made contact with the fire department's dispatch and Rescue was sent to recover Regina's body, while the police officers in East Division combed the streets for Regina's car.

Still, the biggest break in the case was far from the streets they were searching. In fact, it was right under their noses.

12.

Kevin Lynch was anxious after learning that Marilyn had been killed by the car bomb outside the federal building. The news that the city had not been struck by terrorists was good, but Troy Williams had claimed more victims, and that was tragic. With his list now down to Karima, the clock was furiously ticking.

Lynch rushed into Police Headquarters and sprinted off the elevator, moving quickly as he walked into the unkempt Homicide division, with its battered steel furniture and tattered cardboard evidence boxes.

The voice mail that the sergeant had left was cryptic. But if what she'd said was anything close to the truth, the young woman waiting in his office was the key to finding the killer.

"I see you got the voice mail, Captain," the sergeant said as Lynch walked in the door.

"Where is she?" Lynch said, looking around wild-eyed.

The sergeant nodded toward Lynch's closed office door and

indicated that he should follow her. The two of them crossed the room and the sergeant opened Lynch's door slightly.

Lynch looked inside and saw a twentysomething blonde sitting at his desk wearing a red silk dress that left little to the imagination.

The sergeant closed the door before the woman could turn around. "She came to the window downstairs about fifteen minutes ago," the sergeant said. "She told the guy at the desk she could give us Troy Williams and Anthony 'Heads' Porter. At first he just laughed. Then she showed him pictures of her and Heads in, um, compromising positions. A few minutes later, he had a patrolman bring her upstairs.

"I had a couple of detectives spend a few minutes with her, but she said she'd only talk to you."

Lynch nodded. He knew that Chuck's murder provided a link between Heads and Troy Williams. The drugs they'd found at the site of the crash were enough to convince him of that. Lynch's only concern was that the girl wouldn't know enough to truly help them. At this point, he had nothing to lose.

"I'll talk to her, but I'm going to need you to come in with me," he said with a half-smile. "I'm through being alone with young girls."

The sergeant hustled to catch up with the captain as he walked into his office and sat down behind his desk.

"I'm Captain Lynch," he said, flipping through papers and avoiding eye contact with the woman. "This is Sergeant Flowers. How can we help you?"

"I hear you're looking for Anthony Porter," she said, sitting up in her seat and trying to look businesslike. "I can help you."

"Oh, yeah? How's that?" Lynch said as he continued to flip through the papers.

"I'm his girlfriend."

Lynch put the papers down and looked up at the sergeant with an amused expression on his face. Then he looked the girl up and down.

"His girlfriend, huh? Is that what they're calling it these days?"

The girl looked insulted. The sergeant looked amused. Lynch looked the girl in the eye.

"If you're his girlfriend, why are you here?"

Embarrassed, she shifted her gaze from Lynch to the sergeant. Then she looked down in her lap and played with her fingers nervously.

"He, um . . . he's going to meet some other woman."

"What does that have to do with us?" Lynch asked cynically.

"He was on the phone and I heard him say he was meeting this girl at a warehouse at Twentieth and Clearfield. Her name is, um . . . Cream."

In an instant, Lynch's attitude changed.

Standing up, he rounded his desk and stood over her. "Are you sure he said he was going to meet someone named Cream?"

"Yeah," she said, looking from Lynch to the sergeant, her expression that of a frightened child. "That's what I heard him say."

"Do you know why they were meeting?" Lynch asked, his tone frantic.

"I'm not sure. I think he was trying to get her to lead him to this guy Troy Williams. Heads said he was going to kill him for stealing a package from one of his dealers."

"When are they supposed to be meeting at this warehouse?" Lynch asked.

"About a half hour from now."

Lynch grabbed his jacket and ran to the door. "Get this witness's name and get her someplace safe. Then get some plainclothes backup down to that factory. We don't have much time."

The officer in car 2419 had been on the force for nearly fifteen years, and he'd been in the Twenty-fourth District for five.

He knew the tiny streets surrounding K and A better than anyone in the division. So rather than focusing his search for Regina's car on the main streets, he concentrated on the small ones, with their broken-down garages and trash-strewn lots.

He'd already hit Thayer, Cornwall, Willard, and Madison. Now he was down to Shelbourne Street. As he rode slowly toward the end of the block, a group of children playing dodgeball ran in front of his cruiser. Stopping suddenly to avoid hitting them, he watched as the ball bounced into a vacant lot. A little girl picked it up and, in the process, knocked a withered branch from its perch on a late-model car. When the branch fell, the officer saw a shiny patch of red. He looked closer and saw a headlight. Getting out of his car, he walked toward the abandoned lot. He knew before he got there that he'd found what he was looking for.

"This is 2419," he said into his handheld radio. "I've got Regina Brown's car on Shelbourne Street, off Allegheny."

The airwaves came to life, just as he knew they would, as nearly every officer in the division jumped in to say they were on their way.

He didn't respond to the chatter. Instead, he walked over to the children playing dodgeball. "Hi," he said to the little girl who'd recovered the ball from the lot. "What's your name?"

"Katie," she said, her stringy brown hair swinging over her pale face as she regarded him with a shy smile.

She looked to be about six. In another year, she'd lose her innocence and her trust of the police. For now, though, she was all he had, so he questioned her.

"Did you see the man who left that car over there, Katie?" he asked patiently.

She nodded.

"Where'd he go?"

She pointed toward Allegheny Avenue.

"Was it just a few minutes ago?"

"Yes."

"Was he wearing green clothes and a cap?" he asked with a smile.

She nodded.

He was about to ask another question when her mother looked out the window and spotted her talking to him. She ran outside and grabbed her daughter.

"Katie don't know nothin'," the woman snapped, picking up the girl and carrying her home. "Youse ain't gonna protect us when these murderers come back."

The officer watched the woman slam her door and went back to his car as the swelling sound of sirens filled the tiny street.

Five other cars and a wagon pulled up behind his. The other children who'd been playing outside disappeared into their houses. The officer found a sergeant and told him what he knew.

"The job's founded," he said. "Some kids saw him put the car in the lot and walk toward Allegheny Avenue. One little girl said it was in the last few minutes, but she was little, so that could mean anything."

"Still wearing the same clothes?" the sergeant asked as he prepared to transmit the information by radio.

"Yeah, but that might've changed by now."

Static from the old transistor radio filled the one-room apartment where Troy was holed up. It was difficult to understand every word that the reporter was saying, but in between the static, Troy heard the only news that mattered.

"City officials have determined . . . a bomb . . . killing former City Council President Marilyn Johnson and . . . not a terrorist attack . . . KYW news time is three-thirty-five."

With the afternoon nearly gone, Troy had neither the time nor the inclination to celebrate. So he turned off the radio. And then, with the same coldness he'd exhibited while committing eight murders in less than twenty-four hours, he took the list from his back pocket, crossed off Marilyn's name, and circled the final word on the paper—Karima.

He crossed the room quickly and sat in front of the crate that held the laptop he'd used to track down Marilyn. After restarting the GPS program, he punched in Karima's cell phone number and watched as the system searched for nearly two minutes and failed to find a location. Troy hit the REFRESH button. Another two minutes passed, and then he hit the REFRESH button again. Nothing.

Troy slammed his fist against the crate in frustration. He was now twenty minutes behind schedule, and he had no idea where to find his most important target.

He picked up the cell phone he'd packed away with his other supplies and began dialing Karima's number. Thinking better of it, he disconnected the call. He considered sending her a text message, but he knew that would be an equally bad move.

Troy needed to know where Karima was, and he needed to do it without tipping his hand. Looking at the time at the bottom right corner of the computer screen, he saw that it was nearly three-forty. He told himself it was worth it to wait a few more minutes. Anything beyond that would be too risky.

As he hit the REFRESH button again, Troy could sense for the first time in his life the presence of the twin sister he'd never known.

Deep down, he knew that their paths would soon collide. Just as Troy was searching frantically for Karima, he could feel that she was searching desperately for him.

Minimizing the screen that contained the current search, Troy opened another window and logged into Duane's offshore bank account.

At first he thought the information that popped onto the screen was a typo. Then he thought that he was seeing it wrong. When he hit the REFRESH button, he saw the same number in the credit column that he'd seen before—zero.

"Karima," Troy growled through clenched teeth, and his anger quickly grew into uncontrollable rage.

His eyes began darting back and forth. His palms started to

sweat. The hairs on the back of his neck stood on end. As the fury bubbled up from his belly to his mouth, he let loose a primal yell that made him sound almost like an animal.

He picked up the computer, raised it high over his head, and was about to crash it down against the floor when suddenly the last vestiges of his sanity rose up through his madness.

He stood there for a moment, his chest heaving as he looked around the room with eyes the size of saucers. His heartbeat slowed and the rage subsided. Troy gently put the computer down while cursing himself for not draining the account when he had the chance.

With a frustrated sigh, Troy sat down in a heap in front of the computer. Then he took a deep breath and asked himself which was more important—the money, or killing Karima. The answer came from the deepest recesses of his fractured mind: completing what he'd set out to do was the only thing that mattered.

Troy reached into the backpack that contained the supplies for his escape, and he fingered the money he'd saved while working as an FBI profiler. Now that Duane's half-million was gone, Troy would have to live on the twenty thousand.

Karima would pay for that. She would give him every penny of that money back, and then she would die like a dog. Troy would make sure of it.

Reopening the GPS system, he wiped sweat from his forehead as the computer linked to a satellite and a series of towers to trace the GPS chip in Karima's Trio. The wait for the results seemed to take hours. This time, when the browser stopped moving, Karima's location had been pinpointed. For the first time since he'd located Marilyn, Troy smiled.

He shut the laptop, jumped up from his seat, and placed it in the backpack with the other items he needed to complete his final task.

With the car keys in hand and the gun tucked into his waistband, he rushed across the room and looked at his reflection in the chipped mirror over the kitchen sink. Carefully, he glued the fake beard to his face and pulled the hairs so that they extended straight down. He put on the 76ers cap that was at least a size too big, and allowed the shadow from the hat's bill to cover his face.

He looked at his reflection again, and saw someone completely different from the man who'd worked as a profiler for the FBI. The beard, the cap, the oversized T-shirt and jeans made him look like so many other young men who were walking the streets of Philadelphia in the summer heat.

Pulling the backpack onto his shoulder, he grabbed the keys to the Impala he'd parked on nearby H Street in preparation for this moment. Then he moved toward the window and looked out at what he expected to be an empty corner.

What Troy saw on the sidewalk below was a drastic change from a few minutes before. Just as he'd managed to pinpoint Karima's location, the police were gathering at Kensington and Allegheny, in an effort to locate his position.

"It sounded like it came from up there," said the old woman who was standing in the midst of five police officers on the corner of Kensington and Allegheny.

She was pointing to the third floor of the building where Troy was hiding. Like many of the neighbors, she'd seen him go upstairs around three o'clock, and she'd heard his bloodcurdling yell just a few minutes before the police arrived. Unlike those who had long ago stopped paying attention to the madness going on around them, the old woman made a point of observing everything. She'd lived too long to care about the prospect of being labeled a snitch.

"Green work clothes, right?" she asked the sergeant who was running the search.

"That's right," the sergeant said quickly.

"I'm sure, then. He's up there."

The sergeant surveyed the building. There was one entrance in the front and eight windows on each floor—four facing Kensington Avenue, and four facing Allegheny.

"Is there a back entrance?" he asked.

"Yes, but it's locked," the old woman said.

"Thanks, ma'am," he said, thinking for a moment before motioning for one of the officers to take the old woman across the street.

He grabbed his radio and whispered into it. "This is 24A. I need 2400 and 2402 at either end of 1800 Allegheny, and I need 24 Tom 1 and 24 Tom 2 at both ends of 3200 Kensington."

The officers acknowledged the command and moved to block off the streets.

"Radio, send SWAT to this location. We may have a barricaded man situation."

As the dispatcher acknowledged his orders, the sergeant knew he didn't have time to wait for SWAT or anyone else to arrive, so he did what he had to do.

"Jones, I need you and Smith to get the back entrance," he

said. "See if you can open it, but if you can't, just wait there. We don't need to spook this guy with a bunch of noise."

As the two officers jogged to the back of the building, the sergeant and a patrolman went in through the front door and closed it quietly behind them.

They walked inside the vestibule, passing beneath a single flickering lightbulb as they walked into the hallway that led to the stairs.

As the sergeant and the patrolman drew their weapons, the light flickered for the last time and the hallway went dark. They stopped for a moment, trying to allow their eyes to adjust. They didn't have time to wait, so the sergeant tiptoed up the first five steps, believing that Troy had only three options: the front stairs, the back stairs, or the roof.

Though the walls on either side of the staircase prevented the sergeant from seeing anything beyond the landing, he could hear the sounds of muffled soap operas playing behind battered apartment doors. He could hear the couple arguing in the apartment at the middle of the hall. He could hear the thump of a car's stereo from two blocks away, but he couldn't hear Troy coming.

As he rounded the stairs at the landing and started up the second flight, the sergeant tripped and fell. When he looked up, a man in baggy jeans and a T-shirt was standing over him. He spent a split second trying to decide if it was Troy. It was a split second too long.

The sergeant started to stand, and Troy plunged the ice pick into his Adam's apple with one hand while grabbing his gun with the other.

The patrolman ran up the stairs as the sergeant fell back on the landing. When he rounded the wall with his gun out in front of him, the sergeant lay in front of him, gagging on his own blood. The patrolman looked up the stairs just as Troy struck him with the butt of the sergeant's gun. The patrolman's gun fell from his hand as blood spurted from the three-inch gash that opened up near his temple.

He regained his balance and swung as hard as he could. And while he had trouble seeing his target through the blood running into his eye, he somehow connected and knocked Troy backward. The officer rushed forward. Troy bent his legs and pushed off the steps, springing at him with the ice pick, and plunging it so deep into his chest that only the handle was visible.

Troy left both dead men on the landing, grabbed one of the officers' guns, and ran along the second-floor hallway, banging on doors. "Help me!" he said, sounding frantic. "There's a police officer hurt out here!"

In most places, someone would have at least peered out into the hallway. This was K and A, and in this place, there weren't many neighbors who would open their doors for anything short of a fire.

When he banged on the door of the apartment at the end of the hall, there was no response, and Troy couldn't afford to wait for one. He kicked in the door and walked inside, pointing the gun and waiting for someone to emerge from the shadows. No one did. The apartment was empty—just as he'd hoped.

Troy walked to the window and looked down. There were two patrol officers at the back door of the building. And there was a squad of officers dressed in black, wearing helmets and flak jackets, and carrying a battering ram. They would burst through the back door in seconds. When they did, Troy would have little chance of walking out alive.

He stood for half a second, thinking. Then he darted out the door and into the hallway, ran to the place where the fallen officers lay, and pumped two shots into their bodies.

The sound of the gunshots reverberated in the hall. As he ran back into the apartment and shut the door behind him, he heard the sound of the battering ram pounding against the steel of the back door. A thousand shouting voices filled the air. Thundering footsteps shook the front and back stairwells.

Troy climbed out the window and onto the ledge. With his back to the wall, he slid toward the building next door. When he reached the window, he smashed it with the butt of the officers' gun, then reached in and opened it. Scrambling inside, he looked around. He half expected someone to come rushing at him, but the building, like so many others in the area, was abandoned.

Troy moved quickly past the graffiti-covered walls and down the rickety wooden steps. When he reached the front door, he looked across the street and saw the crowd that had formed to watch the confusion, and the police officers who had extended yellow crime scene tape in an effort to hold them back.

Pulling down his cap and putting the officer's stolen handgun into the backpack with his own forty-caliber semiautomatic, he took a deep breath, opened the front door, and walked out into the street. He walked backward, gazing up at the apartment building like some curious onlooker who was smitten by the prospect of seeing a police chase.

It took him thirty steps to make it to the other side of the street. When he did, he literally backed into one of the officers who was charged with crowd control.

"Get outta the way," the cop said, grabbing Troy by the arm and pushing him toward the other side of the tape.

"Oh, my bad," Troy said, abandoning his boarding school diction for the lingo of the streets.

A minute later, with his hat pulled low and his beard firmly in place, Troy melted into the crowd. After a few minutes of watching with the rest of them, he stuffed his hands into his pockets and began walking down Kensington Avenue with his backpack slung over his shoulder. Just as Troy was about to turn the corner onto H Street and get into the old police car he'd bought for the last phase of his plan, he looked up and saw a single cop staring at him.

Troy put his head down and walked faster, hoping that the cop was looking at someone else. When he saw the officer take off his hat and gaze at something inside, Troy moved faster still, knowing that cops kept pictures of wanted people in their hats. When the cop looked up from his hat and placed his hand on the butt of his gun, Troy knew he'd been recognized. He abandoned all caution.

Darting around the corner, Troy got down on the ground and crawled to the car door. When he reached it, he opened the door, hopped inside, sunk low in the driver's seat, and started the car.

He reached up to adjust the rearview mirror. Then he pulled out of the space slowly, watching as the cop rounded the corner and ran into the middle of the street. Troy could see that the cop was looking for a pedestrian. When he didn't find one, he focused on the only thing moving—the car.

The cop yelled something into his radio. Troy gunned the engine. A moment later, as the police scrambled to their cars to pursue him, the airwaves came alive with the news that Troy Williams had been spotted on the street.

13.

Kevin Lynch rode in silence as he approached 20th Street. No lights. No sirens. No warning. Stealth was the only thing that would allow him to disrupt the meeting between Heads and Karima. Hopefully, that same strategy would help him get to Troy before they did.

As he approached the enclave of abandoned factories where Heads's girlfriend said the meeting would take place, an alert tone went out over police radio. What came next changed everything.

"Cars stand by," the dispatcher said quickly. "Twenty-four-nineteen is in pursuit of a black Chevy Impala, traveling north on H Street from Kensington. The occupant is believed to be Troy Williams."

Lynch slowed down as he listened to the Twenty-fourth and Twenty-fifth district officers join the pursuit. As he did, he tried to imagine why Troy would be nearly four miles away when the girlfriend had said he would be at the factory.

The way Lynch figured it, the girlfriend could've lied of her own volition; she could've been lying at Heads's behest; or she could've been sent to Lynch by Troy, as yet another facet of a plan that had thus far worked to perfection.

Lynch wasn't sure if any of those was the right answer. In the back of his mind, he knew that there was yet another possibility: the girlfriend could've been telling the truth. If she was, and Troy was still on his way to the factory, he could be there in as little as ten minutes.

Lynch stopped the car, picked up his BlackBerry, and dialed the Homicide division. "Flowers?" he said when the sergeant answered the phone.

Before he could say anything else, she started telling him about the chase taking place across town.

"I know," he said, pinching his nose between his thumb and forefinger.

She told him that it looked like the girl's story might have been made up, and that she thought Lynch should lead a contingent of detectives to Kensington Avenue for the inevitable end of the pursuit.

Lynch listened to her. He considered it. Then he made a decision that could cost him the case, his job, or his life.

If Flowers was right and the girl had made up the story, the manpower would be deployed where Troy had actually been spotted, not where he might eventually turn up.

"Send every available detective over to Kensington," he said. "I'm on location at the factory, and I'm going to stay here."

"But Captain, what if—"

"Just follow my orders, Sergeant!" he snapped. "We don't have time to argue the point."

There was a moment of silence.

"I'll send them over," Flowers said quietly. "But you're not going into that factory by yourself. I'm coming to back you up."

He started to respond, but she'd already disconnected the call.

Lynch considered calling back, but he needed to get in position. He placed his BlackBerry on the seat and drove to the back of an empty house on the south side of the factory.

When he got out, he saw a large figure walking toward the back of the factory, carrying a small briefcase. Lynch ducked into the shadows of the dilapidated house and watched as the man turned around to see if anyone was behind him. Lynch saw his face. It was Heads, which meant that the meeting was going forward as planned.

Lynch disappeared into the house and made his way up the rickety stairs so he could get a better view of the street. As he looked out the broken window and watched for more activity, he knew that it would all come down to Troy.

If he was caught before he walked into Heads's and Karima's meeting, then Lynch had gambled and lost, but Lynch's gut told him that Troy wouldn't be apprehended.

The sound of screaming sirens filled the air as the black Chevy Impala skidded onto Westmoreland Street with police cars weaving in and out of traffic to catch it.

Troy looked in the mirror as he pressed the accelerator to the floor, clipped the right side of a car in front of him, and veered onto the sidewalk, barely missing a group of playing children.

As he sped toward G Street, a police car pulled into the intersection, blocking his path. He swerved right to avoid it, fishtailing as his rear bumper smacked the front of the police car.

There was a popping sound behind him as the cop jumped out of the damaged car and began to shoot. Troy slumped down in his seat, the rear window of the black Impala exploding in a hail of glass as a bullet lodged in the dashboard. When it did, he felt a sharp pain on his left side.

Troy began to zigzag in the hopes of avoiding the gunfire. As he did, he heard the familiar *thump* of helicopter blades above him. With the police tracking him from the air, his chances of escaping were rapidly evaporating, but Troy wasn't one to give up.

He slammed the brakes, whipped the steering wheel right, and swerved onto Ontario Street at sixty miles per hour. There were screams as people dove to get out of the street. There was the sickening smell of burning rubber as tires skidded against asphalt. There was the renewed sound of sirens as two police cars took up the chase.

Troy heard none of it. As he turned left onto I Street, the only thing he heard was the sound his last victim would make when he killed her. It was that sound that drove him. In pursuit of that sound, he spotted his means of escape.

The police cars behind him closed in rapidly as he drove toward the strip mall with the liquor stores and the day care center. When he turned his steering wheel and stomped the accelerator to the floor, heading straight for the parking lot where parents were beginning to pick up their children, he did so with one intention—escaping.

A second before the Impala crashed through the front window of the liquor store, Troy opened the door of the car, held his backpack in front of him, and jumped.

He rolled on the ground as the car crashed through the window and burst into flames. While the heat from the fire kept the police from running in, he crawled through the smoke and chaos, looking for a way out. Just as he was ready to give up, he found it.

A young mother came running out of the day care center with her four-year-old son in tow. He watched her face as she ran to save her car from the impending explosion. He could see that she had only two things in the world—her son and her car. She was determined to save them both.

Troy was determined, too. He climbed through the back door of the unlocked car and saved the only thing in his life that mattered—himself.

The woman opened the front door, threw the boy into the passenger seat and got behind the wheel. Then, as billowing smoke and heat from the burning vehicle kept police officers at bay, the woman put her car in reverse and, like so many others who'd run from the building, sped from the parking lot. No one stopped her. No one could have. Seconds after she rounded the corner with her son safely beside her, the car that Troy had driven into the wall exploded.

Three minutes later, when they were far away from the scene where the police believed they would find his body, Troy rose up slowly from the car's back seat and stuck the gun in the boy's face.

The woman shrieked and slammed on the brakes, and the car skidded to a stop. As the boy began to cry, Troy put a finger to his lips, silencing both of them. When they calmed down, he took off his backpack with one hand as pain shot through his side. Ignoring the pain, he took out his laptop and opened it.

As he opened the GPS program to recheck Karima's location, his voice filled the car.

"You're taking me across town," he said evenly. "And if you do anything to keep me from getting there, your son is going to die."

"He's close," Karima said, shuddering as she prepared to get out of the car with Skeet and Mr. Vic.

"How you know?" Skeet asked as he watched her from the back seat.

"He's my twin," Karima said as she surveyed their grim surroundings and drank in every detail. "I can feel him."

Neither Skeet nor Mr. Vic responded. Both of them knew what she meant, especially Skeet.

He'd spent every moment since they'd left the speakeasy watching her. In that time, his heart had confirmed what his mind already knew. She was the sister he'd never had, the kindred spirit he'd never known. The two of them were meant to be together in this moment, at this place, in this time.

He recognized that the bond between them was stronger than he could have imagined, though he also realized that he envied her. She would, after all, have an opportunity that he never could—the chance to avenge her mother's death. For that chance, Skeet would've gladly given up the money he stood to gain. Even with the money, he now knew what he didn't want to do. He didn't want any of them to come out of this alone.

"Let's go," Mr. Vic said, breaking into his thoughts.

Skeet put a hand on his shoulder. "Wait."

Both the old man and Karima turned around.

"Karima, whatever happen, I want you to know you ain't gon' be by yourself," Skeet said. "Not now. Not ever. 'Cause we your family now."

Karima was about to respond, but her phone beeped, signaling a text message.

They all looked at one another. Then Karima took the phone out of her purse and reluctantly pushed the button that would display the text message. When she saw it, she reached into her bag and took out the gun she'd gotten from Mr. Vic.

"What it say?" Skeet asked anxiously.

Karima placed a finger against her lips. Then she held up the phone for both of them to see: *Come out, come out, wherever you are.*

Karima dropped her purse to the floor as she chambered a round with a double *click*. Skeet and Mr. Vic pulled their guns and held them out in front of them with their fingers on the triggers. All of them searched the desolate street, in hopes of spotting Troy before he spotted them.

"In ten minutes, we meet back here," Mr. Vic said as he eased the car door open. "If anything go wrong, do whatever you gotta do to make it out."

Lynch watched from the abandoned house at the end of the block as the three of them emerged from the old Cadillac.

The old man got out first, walking toward the factory with his gun pointed toward the ground. A teenaged boy emerged from the car and walked toward the factory with a gun in his hand. Karima exited last.

When Lynch watched her get out of the car with a gun in her hand, he braced himself for a flood of emotion. It never came. He simply watched her like he did the others—with a cool detachment that was fueled by his desire to capture the killer and close the case.

Gone was the lust he'd felt for her just hours before. It had been replaced by apprehension spurred by one undeniable fact— Karima might not make it out of this alive.

Lynch wished he could go to her and convince her to stop. He wished he could tell her that it wasn't worth her life. The reality was, he couldn't. Lynch had to catch a killer, and he couldn't do that if the killer didn't show. He decided to maintain his position, and cradled the handheld radio whose volume he'd reduced to near-silence.

Placing it against his ear, he listened to the chatter from the cops in the Twenty-fourth District, and his best hopes and worst fears were simultaneously confirmed. They hadn't found Troy in the wreckage near the liquor store, and though they had no idea where to look, Lynch did.

He gripped his weapon tightly as he surveyed the street, looking for the man whom he knew would soon arrive. Then he reached down and switched the radio to M Band—the frequency most often used by detectives and other special units.

The first voice he heard was that of Sergeant Flowers. "Dan Fifteen, on location," she said as she pulled up at the end of the block.

"Meet me on the south side of the factory, near Toronto Street," he whispered into the radio. "Use caution. We're still waiting for Troy."

Flowers acknowledged the order before moving into position. Just as she and the captain walked onto the factory grounds, another car made its way toward the block.

"Turn here," Troy said, checking his cell phone to make sure that his text message had gone through.

The woman did as she was told, steering with one hand and wiping her tears with the other as they arrived at the corner of 19th and Clearfield.

She glanced at her four-year-old, who wept silently in the passenger seat.

"Please," she said, her fear pouring out in tears. "Don't hurt my son. I'll do anything you say."

Troy sneered as he pressed the gun against the boy's head. "Anything?"

"Whatever you want," she said, her words barely audible between sobs.

"Go around the corner and park on Lippincott Street."

Without hesitation, she turned onto the tiny street and pulled over with the engine running. "It's gonna be all right, baby," she said to her son, though she'd really said it to reassure herself.

"Yeah, it's gonna be all right," Troy said, his words slurring and his eyes closing slightly as the pain in his side grew sharper. "In a few minutes, it's all gonna be all right."

The woman heard the change in his voice, and she looked in the rearview mirror, examining his eyes before looking down at his T-shirt. It was stained dark red on the lower left-hand side, and though he held his hand against it, she could see the thick red blood that was seeping out between his fingers.

"You're bleeding!" she said, sounding alarmed.

He smiled and winced at the same time. "Cops got a lucky shot—nothing a couple of stitches can't heal."

"Let me get you some help," the woman said, sounding as desperate as she looked. "My son and I, we can—"

"Strip," he said, sitting up straight and staring at her over the seat.

The woman shook her head slowly from side to side. "Please— not in front of my son," she said, her voice quaking.

"Do it now or the boy dies."

"But I—"

"Now!" Troy shouted, his breath coming fast and heavy as the blood leaked steadily from the gunshot wound in his side.

The woman took off her skirt and blouse, and was about to remove her bra and panties when Troy raised his hand. "Get out," he said quietly. "Take your son and walk to Twenty-second Street. Don't look back."

By now she knew better than to protest, so she grabbed the boy by the hand, got out of the car, and walked past a row of ramshackle houses and closed factories, heading toward the busy commercial strip on 22nd Street. There, she would get all the attention a nearly naked woman would command in the heart of North Philadelphia. And Troy would have the perfect diversion he'd need to take care of his business.

Easing out of the back seat, he got behind the wheel of the car, drove the wrong way down Lippincott Street, turned onto 20th, and pulled along the edge of the four-foot-high cinderblock wall that ran from the factory to the nearby train tracks. He knew that he couldn't stop now. The GPS system had confirmed her location. The text message he'd sent from the back seat of the car had been delivered. Now he had only to finish what he'd begun.

Wincing with pain from the bullet in his side, Troy left everything in the car except a gun, ammunition, and an ice pick. He had no need for anything else now.

He climbed gingerly over the cinderblock wall and started through the weeds on the north side of the factory.

When he saw her, he would make Karima pay for her life of privilege and his life of pain.

She'd lived like she was the angel of the Thomas clan, with access to the money their grandfather had left to Sharon, and a birthright that made her the heir apparent to the family's political power. She'd benefited from the financial support that their father, Bill Johnson, had provided, and from the love that Sharon tried to give.

Troy, on the other hand, had lived his life as if he were a demon who was exiled from the family he never knew: bouncing from one foster home to another, never knowing the love of his parents, suffering at the hands of abusers.

Today, they were going to switch places. Karima would be the demon to be exiled. Troy would be the angel of death.

After Mr. Vic went in, Skeet crossed 20th Street, passing over asphalt-covered trolley tracks to get to the factory whose broken windows and empty air conditioner holders gave it the appearance of a pockmarked face.

Squeezing between the rusty iron plates that blocked the old factory's entrance on the west side of the building, he moved between trailers and overflowing Dumpsters. He avoided the piles of rubble where addicts shot heroin and smoked crack. He walked through weeds where old diapers and used condoms had been discarded.

Fifty yards in front of him, an old smokestack stood with a crack running up the side of its crumbling brick face. To his left, there were weeds the size of trees. To his right, there was an entrance to the factory. But he didn't go inside until he saw Mr. Vic wave from behind the smokestack, and Karima make her way through the rusted iron plates to take her place behind him.

With everyone in position, Skeet walked into the factory and looked for Troy. He also looked to assure himself that Heads had traveled as he normally did—alone.

The more he looked, the less likely it seemed that either of them had shown up. It was difficult to know if things were as they seemed, because the forgotten factory—like all the closed factories around it—contained too many hiding places.

Skeet zigzagged through an obstacle course of debris in an attempt to search every dark place on the factory floor. As he did, he could smell the thick scent of mold from the rain that had fallen through holes in the roof. Then, as he searched among the clutter of rusted machines that had been stripped of every valuable piece of scrap metal, he noticed a dark figure watching his every move. He was large and forbidding, just like the building. As Skeet looked around once more, he could tell one more thing. He was alone.

"Where Cream at?" Heads said as he began the long walk across the factory floor.

"Right here," Karima said, appearing, as if by magic, at Skeet's side.

Heads stopped for a moment. Then he took slow, deliberate steps toward them, the outline of his body only slightly darker than the dimly lit space around him. Occasionally, he hit a patch of the sunlight that streamed down through the damaged roof. It revealed quick flashes of the man beneath the shadows, but it wasn't enough to reveal the whole truth.

As he got closer, his silhouette grew larger. When finally he emerged from the shadows and stood before them, he appeared to be bigger than life.

He stood there for a moment, staring at Karima with unbridled lust in his eyes. Karima stared back at him, her expression revealing grief and resolve. She looked him in the eye and allowed vulnerability to show through. It was as if she'd already given herself over to his protection. He liked that. It made him feel powerful. That was exactly where she wanted him.

"All right, Skeet," he said, still staring hungrily at Karima. "You can wait outside. I'll call you when I need you."

Without a backward look, the boy did as he was told. He left the factory the same way he'd come in. A few seconds later, when he was sure that his boss had given Karima his full attention, he circled around to meet Mr. Vic in the back.

"So where the package you was supposed to be bringin'?" Heads said, grinning at Karima in spite of himself.

"On his way," she said easily.

Karima could tell that the wheels in his head were turning. She could almost hear his suspicions bubbling up to the surface.

Heads was tense. The factory was still. Karima was starting to get nervous.

Suddenly, something scurried across the floor behind Heads. With lightning quickness for a man his size, he reached into his waistband, pulled out a Glock, and spun around while pointing the gun. As his eyes darted back and forth and his finger tightened on the trigger, a rat walked away from the pile of trash where it had been rummaging. Heads eased his grip on the weapon.

He was sweating when he turned around to face Karima, and he wasn't happy that his nerves had gotten the best of him. "Where the fuck that dude at?" he said while stuffing the gun back into his waistband.

Karima wanted to spit in his face, but she managed a shy grin instead.

"Where's the money?" she asked sweetly.

"You'll see the money when I see the dude that took my shit," he said aggressively.

She smiled again, trying to buy time until Skeet and Mr. Vic could meet and circle around to the back of the factory floor. As far as Heads was concerned, her time had already run out.

He moved toward her suddenly, putting his arms around her and feeling the small of her back. Karima knew she couldn't fight him, so she relaxed, knowing what he would find.

"What's this?" he asked as he removed her gun from the back of her waistband and held it up between them.

"I don't move on the streets without protection," she said quietly. "You shouldn't, either."

She looked over his shoulder as if she were communicating

with someone behind him. As soon as she did that, Heads knew he'd been set up.

He reached out to grab her, but she ducked. He turned around with both Karima's gun and his own gun in his hands, aiming at his unseen assailant. Before he could get a shot off, two shots rang out from the shadows. One bullet missed badly, hitting a piece of old factory equipment. The other punched into Heads's skull and exploded from the back of his head, spraying blood-soaked gray matter on Karima and everything around her.

For a moment, she sat on the floor, unable to move as she tried to figure out where the shots had come from. When Mr. Vic came stumbling out of the shadows, she sprang to her feet and grabbed her gun from Heads's dead fingers.

"Where's Skeet?" she asked frantically.

Mr. Vic didn't answer. He simply grabbed her and pushed her behind a piece of machinery before turning and squeezing off a shot that ricocheted off the back wall.

Karima looked out from behind the machine and aimed her gun in the same direction, but she didn't see anything. A second later, when she took cover and looked at Mr. Vic, his face was twisted in pain, and blood seeped out of a puncture wound in the back of his neck.

"Troy did this to you?" she whispered as she watched the old man dying her mother's death.

Mr. Vic nodded as three quick shots were fired from the other side of the factory.

"I'm getting you out of here," she said, dragging him close to her while looking out from behind the machine in search of some sign of her brother.

The old man coughed and smiled through excruciating pain. "I told you if I died I wanted to know I did at least one thing right." He looked up into her eyes. "Helpin' you was that thing. Now you gotta finish it. I'ma just . . . stay here . . . and rest."

Mr. Vic's eyes closed and his breath slowed down. Karima cradled his head in her arms, just like she'd done her mother. As she held him, his breathing became labored and ragged. In less than a minute, it had stopped.

"Troy!" Karima yelled through tears of grief and rage. "This is between you and me! Come out now so we can finish it!"

As Karima's words echoed through the building, Troy began to laugh. It was quiet at first, as if he were trying not to let her hear. Then it was louder, more uproarious, arrogant.

Troy shuffled forward from the shadows in the back of the room. He had his forearm firmly wrapped around Skeet's neck as he marched the boy out like a human shield.

"You say it's between us, but you send a boy and an old man to do your work for you," Troy said, his thin voice bouncing off the factory walls. "You send a two-bit drug dealer to kill me. I'm not surprised, though. That's just like the Thomases," he said as the blood ran out of his wounded side. "Let someone else do the heavy lifting, right, Karima? Let someone else raise the boy we don't want. He can rot, as far as we're concerned. We're Thomases! It's all about us."

His voice was weak. When Karima peered out from behind the machine, she could see why. What had started as a trickle was a full-fledged river of blood that ran down the side of his T-shirt and drenched one side of his jeans.

With Heads's dead body the only thing between them and

Skeet being held as a virtual prisoner, Karima knew what she had to do. She ducked behind the machine and put her gun in the back of her waistband.

Before she could come out and lay her life on the line, Kevin Lynch yelled out from somewhere on Karima's right as he and Sergeant Flowers converged on Troy from two different angles.

"Police!" Lynch said, walking out from the shadows with his gun extended in front of him. "Let the boy go, Troy. We can get that wound treated and you can live. Or you can try to hold out and die. Either way, this place is going to be flooded with cops in about one minute. By then, we won't have much choice."

Troy coolly looked at both cops and tightened his grip on Skeet's neck. "There's always a choice," he said, jamming the gun against the boy's head. "And here's yours. Put the guns down or I'll kill him."

Lynch looked at Flowers, who shook her head quickly. Neither had a clean shot at Troy, but they knew that if they relinquished their weapons, the boy would die anyway.

"I said put them down!" Troy said, firing a shot over Lynch's head.

It was then that all hell broke loose.

Both Lynch and Flowers returned fire, hitting Troy in the arm as Skeet wriggled away and ran toward the back of the factory.

Troy fell to the ground and fired at both cops again, emptying a full clip and pinning them down before stopping to reload.

Karima dashed out from behind the machine, firing her gun and screaming as she ran straight at him. When Troy managed to get the clip into the butt of the gun, he turned and fired a kill shot at point-blank range.

The gun jammed. Karima sneered and slowly raised her gun to his head.

"Karima, wait!" Lynch said, running across the room in an effort to stop her. "Don't!"

This was a moment that had been set in motion from the time they were born. Karima looked down at her only brother, and even through the tears that welled up in her eyes, she saw things more clearly than she ever had.

"This is for our mother," she said calmly. "May she rest in peace, and may you burn in hell."

Lynch was almost upon her when she fired the first shot. As Troy's life leaked out in a red stream, she fired another. When he was still, she fired a third.

She stood over him with her chest heaving and the gun dangling from her trigger finger. Lynch approached her from the side and gently took the gun from her hand. Karima didn't resist. She simply waited for Lynch to do what he must. Then something moved in the back of the factory.

When Karima, Lynch, and Flowers looked up to see what it was, three shots rang out, forcing all of them to the floor. Both Lynch and Flowers rolled right, taking cover behind a nearby machine and pointing their weapons toward the source of the gunshots.

Karima crawled to the left, finding another machine to shield her from the next two bullets that were fired. There was a slight pause before another shot hit one of the old machines behind her. A spark flew as the bullet ricocheted. It caught a pile of trash a few feet away, and ignited.

"Put the weapon down and come out now!" Lynch yelled.

There was no response. The trash continued to burn, the flames began to leap, and the crackling sound of the blaze echoed off the factory's walls as the air quickly filled with black smoke.

It was more difficult to see now, and becoming even harder to breathe. Karima coughed as she peered around the machine and looked into the darkness. Just barely visible in the dilapidated building's dim light was Skeet, taking hold of the cash-filled briefcase that Heads had left in the back of the factory. He was raising his gun to fire at Lynch and Flowers again, but Karima waved her hand, begging him to stop. He did.

Still unable to see where the shots had come from, Lynch and Flowers crawled out from their hiding place and started moving toward the back of the factory. Neither of them spoke for fear of giving up their position.

Skeet, with his younger eyes, had already spotted them. He picked up the briefcase and circled around them, moving silently through the black smoke until he reached Karima.

The sound of sirens filled the air outside as police cars and fire vehicles started to arrive. The noise covered the sound of Skeet's coughing as he took Karima by the hand and guided her through the smoke.

They moved toward the edge of the factory, trying desperately to muffle their coughing as they made their way outside.

When they reached the four-foot cinderblock wall that ran along the edge of the factory, Karima tried to stop. Skeet wouldn't let her.

He looked up at the woman he'd come to love as a sister. Then he took her by the hand and they ran behind the cinderblock wall, hidden by the weeds that led to the train tracks.

They ran from the past that had trapped them for so long, and the hopelessness that had marked their existence. They ran for their mothers. They ran for their fathers. They ran for themselves.

They ran knowing that they would someday return to the place where they'd snatched their freedom. They'd return and finish taking the only thing they had left—payback.